BEHIND THE WIRE

A DAN TAYLOR NOVEL

RACHEL AMPHLETT

SAXON
PUBLISHING

ONE

Essaouria, Morocco

Dan Taylor picked up the motor sports magazine, tapped it to his forehead in salute to the café owner, and stepped out into the harsh North African summer, unaware he was being followed.

A momentary shiver ran through his body as he adjusted to the heat after the chill of the air-conditioned café. The awning over the footpath offered little shelter as the sun cresting the rooftops opposite cast a fierce light over the narrow street.

He stood to one side to let a pair of tourists walk past, both carrying surf boards, their American-accented voices fading as their sun-bleached heads bobbed out of view amongst the throng lining the pavement.

A woman stepped off the path and pushed the door to the bakery next to the café open, the fragrant scent of freshly made pastries and bread filling the air.

Dan dropped his sunglasses over his eyes and jogged across the busy street to a convenience store.

He checked his watch.

He was due back at the harbour within the hour. Any later, and the man he'd contacted to provide a new fuel pump for the boat would disappear, and he'd have to spend another month convincing him to return.

He pushed open the door to the shop and made his way towards the lone refrigerator that stood against the back wall, its motor mimicking a death rattle as it fought a losing battle against the summer temperatures.

He grabbed a two-litre plastic container of milk and a bottle of water and joined the short queue at the counter.

The port town had become a favourite haunt of his; until recently, there had been fewer tourists than Casablanca or Fez, so anyone looking for him would stand out in a crowd.

He wasn't a gambling man, though, and so as he

waited in line, his gaze swept the street beyond the dirty windows.

He'd noticed a distinct increase in the number of tourists over the past six months, testament to the fact that at least two UK budget airlines had added the small Moroccan resort to their regular flight schedules, and decided it would soon be time to move on again.

It would be too dangerous to venture further south along the African coast, especially for someone trying to keep a low profile. Instead, he quite liked the idea of crossing the Atlantic and exploring the Caribbean islands for the summer, and he made a mental note to speak to the other boat owners at the marina. If another boat planned to head west soon, he'd find out if he could tag along.

A bus rumbled past and stopped a few metres from the shop. As it belched diesel fumes into the street, its passengers waited with bored faces while others climbed on, the screens of their phones held up to their faces as they tried to ignore the monotony of their journey.

Brakes creaked, the engine revved, and the bus moved on, and Dan's attention returned to the man behind the counter.

He smiled and held up the milk and water.

'How are you, Mr Dan?' The shopkeeper grinned, revealing a mouth devoid of three front teeth, the remainder nicotine-stained.

'Good, Farouk.' Dan indicated the meagre purchases. 'Just these today.'

Dan paid, nodded his thanks, and stepped back out into the morning heat.

The harbour was a fifteen-minute walk from the convenience store, and by the time he reached his destination, sweat pooled between his shoulder blades and over his chest.

The wind changed direction, bringing with it the pungent stink of the fishing boats from the working harbour further along the stretch of *sqalas* – esplanades fortified with ramparts, evidence of the port town's Moroccan rulers implementing Portuguese design several decades ago.

The boats had been in for hours, their produce already sold in the markets, but gulls hovered over the masts, seeking out scraps of food as nets were repaired and the boats readied for the following morning.

Dan reached the entrance gate to the marina as the mobile phone in his pocket began to ring.

He cursed under his breath and ran through his mind all the threats he'd use on the parts supplier if the fuel pump were delayed again. He shifted the bag of shopping into one hand, pushed against the steel mesh gate that led to the concrete jetty, and pulled his phone from his pocket.

'Hello?'

The metallic *clang* of the gate falling back into place obliterated the caller's voice, and Dan glanced at the screen.

Caller unknown.

He tried again. 'Hello?'

'Long time, no speak, Dan.'

He almost dropped the phone and his shopping in shock.

He pivoted on his toes, surveying the boats that bobbed against the jetty, before he narrowed his eyes at the harbour master's office and buildings beyond.

The place was deserted, save for a boy of about twelve fishing at the water's edge.

'David? How the bloody hell did you get this number?'

His mind raced.

He'd been careful, abandoning every aspect of his old life, even going as far as having his boat re-registered in Marseilles before sailing towards the Moroccan coastline, zig-zagging across the Mediterranean under cover of darkness.

After that, he'd kept his head down, telling any

locals he'd befriended since his arrival that he was a former executive, tired of the city rat-race, while he regrouped and tried to figure out what to do next with his life.

His mouth dry, he gripped the phone tighter.

'How the hell did you find me?'

'I'll explain later. We've got a problem.'

'Sort it out yourselves. I'm retired.'

'Bored, more like,' said David Ludlow, a note of contempt underlying his calm tone.

Dan placed the bag on the ground between his feet, and then straightened and scratched at the stubble on his cheek while he tried to formulate an appropriate response in his mind.

His former boss interrupted his thoughts.

'Got a job for you. No time to waste. Might even get you in the good books with the new Prime Minister.'

'New Prime Minister?'

'You do read something other than the sports section of the newspapers?'

Dan bit back the retort on his lips and instead did a quick mental calculation.

'I must've been at sea when it happened.'

'Right.' David sounded unconvinced. 'So you've only been checking the football scores for the past two weeks, then?'

'Wait.' Dan held up his hand and then sighed. 'How did you know where to find me?'

'Hi, Dan.'

He closed his eyes and cursed under his breath. 'Mel?'

The analyst giggled at the end of the line.

'Bloody hell,' said Dan. 'You put a tracker on the boat, didn't you?' He frowned. 'Hang on. If you've known all along where I am, how come I haven't been dragged back there and arrested?'

'Because we haven't told anyone where you are,' said David. 'Which brings me to the matter at hand.'

'David? I'm standing here in ninety degree heat, and the milk for my coffee is about to turn into butter. Like I said, I'm not interested.'

Dan ended the call, picked up his bag, and stalked towards his boat, swearing profusely.

The good mood he'd had since he'd woken up that morning had disappeared, replaced with frustration and a seething anger that, despite everything, David thought it was okay to phone up out of the blue and demand his help.

'Screw that,' he muttered.

Dan forced a smile and raised his hand in greeting as he passed a 32-foot wooden-hulled ketch, her German owners enjoying a lazy brunch under a dark blue shade-cloth.

He swallowed, his throat parched as he envisaged the brew he'd make as soon as he returned to the relative coolness of his own vessel.

Despite the heat, the harbour allowed a little more of the Atlantic's cooling winds to reach its residents, away from the closeness of the town's sprawling buildings.

He trudged on along the jetty and tried to ignore the bead of sweat that ran between his shoulder blades, despite the cotton short-sleeved shirt he wore. His sandals saved his feet from being scorched by the hot concrete surface under his soles, yet even those were beginning to wear thin as the summer progressed.

He stopped at the end of the jetty, crouched down, and began to untie the rope that held his dinghy in place as it bobbed on the gentle waves that splashed against the rubber-hulled vessel.

He straightened, tugged his baseball cap lower over his eyes, and as he lowered his hand, jerked to a standstill.

His boat was fifty metres or so from where he stood, but even at this distance he could see the wheelhouse door swing open with the slight rocking of the boat in the water.

His hand fell to his pocket, and in the split second his fingers found his keys, his other hand dropped his shopping bag to the floor and wrapped around the gun tucked into his waistband that had been concealed under his t-shirt.

'Shit,' he muttered.

First, a phone call out of the blue from David.

Now this.

He inched forward, his eyes tracking the rowing boats that lined this part of the harbour. He'd deliberately moored his vessel at this end – it was quieter, and away from prying eyes.

He glanced over his shoulder.

The German couple's yacht was too far behind him to call to them, to find out if they'd seen anyone suspicious-looking hanging around.

He reasoned that they would have said something to him as he'd walked past. That was simply what boat people did. You spent your life drifting from one port to the next, marina to marina, often crossing dangerous waters, and so you looked out for each other.

He'd only started to pull the dinghy closer to the jetty to climb into it when a single white flash tore through the wheelhouse of his boat.

Dan threw himself to the ground as the air around him was sucked towards the explosion, before the ensuing flames devoured the available oxygen and spat out a ferocious fireball.

He sensed the shockwave pass over his body and put his arms over his head.

Splinters of timber and fibreglass peppered the jetty as the roar of the explosion died away, only to be replaced with the vicious crackling of flames.

Dan raised his head and then ducked as a secondary explosion ripped through the fuel tanks.

'Shit.'

He rose into a crouch and, once satisfied no limbs were broken, stood on shaking legs and surveyed the damage.

It didn't take long.

Within a minute, the first burning remnants of his late father's boat began to sink below the water line.

As the ringing in his ears subsided a little, he became aware of the sound of running feet.

He spun round, ready to fight, before he realised it was only the other residents from the boats in the harbour running towards him, their faces full of concern.

He slipped his gun back into his waistband and tugged his t-shirt down.

'Dan? *Mein gott.*' The German man ran his hands through his hair, his face stricken as he watched the pieces of the boat smoking on the waves. 'Are you okay?'

'I'm okay. Thanks, Markus.'

'You're insured, yes?'

'I think so,' said Dan, and then frowned as he tried to calculate whether the policy had expired in his absence from the UK. 'Maybe.'

Within moments, a small crowd had gathered, and, despite his best efforts to get them to move back to the relative safety of their own boats, they resisted, offering him advice, condolences and, in the case of one rich American widow, a roof over his head – with benefits.

When his phone rang, he answered it with relief and excused himself from the throng.

He walked a few paces back towards the direction of the harbour master's office.

'Hello?'

'Are you okay?' asked David, his voice laden with concern.

Dan bit back the first comment that came to mind and took a calming breath before he spoke.

'Apart from losing a favourite part of my inheritance? Yes. I'm fine. How did you know?'

'Satellite feed,' said Mel.

Dan turned and looked at the smoking mess

that had been his home. 'There are nicer ways to get me to come back and work for you, David.'

'It wasn't us,' said David. 'Anyone else you've managed to piss off? Apart from the British government?'

'Where do I start?' said Dan, knowing the sarcasm in his voice would reach all the way to wherever David had based himself this time.

'Right, well,' said David, 'given that you're now homeless, perhaps you'd like to reconsider my offer?'

'You don't waste time, do you?' Dan's eyes found the rich American woman, who waggled her fingers at him, then pulled her sunglasses down her nose and cocked her eyebrow.

He shook his head to clear the thought that threatened to thwart common sense and began to stalk along the jetty, away from the disaster that had been his boat. He removed his sunglasses and rubbed his eyes. Replacing his sunglasses, he switched the phone to his other hand and ran his fingers through his hair.

'David? Why me? Why now?'

The other man paused, the silence stretching out over the miles until he finally spoke.

'General Collins's daughter is missing in Moroccan-occupied Western Sahara.'

'Anna?'

Dan had last seen Anna several years ago as she was starting her last year of university in Arizona. He recalled a young, leggy blonde who was destined to break all her male classmates' hearts.

'How – how's the general?' he managed.

'At his wits' end,' said David. 'And given the sort of friends he has, and the sort of firepower available to him, you can probably work out for yourself why Her Majesty's Government is keen to avoid him being directly involved in any search and rescue operation.'

'Hell, yes.'

The general ran a highly organised and extremely capable team of private military contractors. Dan couldn't imagine what David and his colleagues could have said to the general to ensure he didn't arrive in Africa with all guns blazing, but it surely couldn't last.

'Does he know you're talking with me?' Dan asked.

'You were his idea,' said David drily. 'Actually, you were more his ultimatum,' he added. 'Something to the effect of "get Dan Taylor there or I'll go myself" – you get the picture.'

'Fine,' Dan said. 'Let's talk.'

'Meet us at the Argan Hotel in twenty minutes,' said David.

'I'll be there.'

'Great,' said Mel. 'I'll put the kettle on, shall I?'

'Very funny.' Dan ended the call and pushed his way past the trickle of people that were walking towards the site of his boat.

In the distance, the forlorn siren tone of the town's singular fire truck grew closer.

A man, local by the look of his clothing and sun-wrinkled skin, held up his hand and stopped Dan in his tracks.

'Where is Englishman?'

'That's me,' said Dan, his senses alert.

The man grinned and held up a cardboard box.

'New fuel pump.' He beamed and thrust a clipboard and pen at Dan. 'One hundred dollars, on delivery. Sign here.'

Dan blinked at the courier and then glanced over his shoulder at the far end of the jetty as the last remnant of his boat sank beneath the waves.

'I don't suppose you offer refunds, do you?'

TWO

Three hours west of Laâyoune, Moroccan-occupied Western Sahara

Anna Collins wrenched open the sliding door of the mini-bus before the driver had brought the vehicle to a standstill and jumped to the ground, her sneakers kicking up a small cloud of dust as she landed.

She pushed back a strand of blonde hair that had escaped her ponytail and shielded her eyes from the glare of the sun on the vehicle's white paintwork before slipping her sunglasses on.

Shrugging her backpack over one shoulder, she waited impatiently while her colleague, Benji, clambered from the vehicle, gathered his laptop to his chest, and slammed the door shut.

The vehicle took off along the road as if the driver were taking part in the Dakar Rally, his pockets fat with the more than adequate compensation they'd negotiated with him for his last-minute diversion.

Anna swallowed as she saw the panic in Benji's eyes.

Sweat poured from his brow, and she no longer wondered if he was as scared as she.

He fumbled in his jeans pocket for a second and withdrew his phone.

'Still nothing,' he said.

Anna shifted from foot to foot, trying to force her heartbeat to slow. She'd managed to speak briefly to her father before they'd left the mine office, telling him that she held grave concerns for hers and Benji's security, but until she could tell him they had reached safety, she couldn't rest. She had to get them both out of the country – and fast.

'Okay,' she managed, and ran her tongue over her lips. 'Let's go to our rooms, pack, and get to the airport. I'll meet you by the car. Fifteen minutes?'

Benji nodded and glanced over his shoulder, back in the direction of where they'd travelled from the new phosphate mine that was being built. 'Are you sure about this?'

'Absolutely,' said Anna. 'You saw the same data as me. We're in trouble.'

Benji cursed, a low hiss escaping between his teeth. 'Okay. Let's pack.'

They shouldered their bags in unison and hurried towards the temporary structures that comprised the mining camp set up for the construction phase of the new development.

The announcement of the discovery of a new phosphate deposit had brought workers from far and wide, desperate to earn good money from the mine. Although touted as a way to encourage the local Sahrawi people into employment and improve their prospects, in truth it was mostly ex-pat Moroccan workers who filled many of the roles on offer, eager to send more money home over the border.

The workers were housed in the main part of the mining camp, a sprawling metropolis of square cabins that resembled shipping containers stacked three high, towering over their occupants as they traipsed to and from work at sunrise and sunset.

Foreign nationals – the Westerners from the mining company and their guests – were housed in more luxurious accommodation at the front of the main camp.

Anna led the way through the small patchy garden that had been planted by some of the workers near the entrance to the reception building, her mind working in overdrive as she tried to contain her fear.

Running would only draw attention, and they couldn't risk that – not yet.

Before they reached the coolness of the reception block, they turned right and passed through an archway.

Beyond, yellow grass and scrubby trees framed a collection of twelve bungalows; concrete and tin roof structures that offered running water and air conditioning, perfect for the use of the client's management and guests such as Anna and Benji who were working at the mine on short-term stays.

'Wait,' said Benji, grabbing Anna's arm. 'Before we split up.'

'What?' She frowned as he rummaged in the side of his laptop case.

He held out a USB stick. 'Take this. It's everything we found out. You know the important stuff, the codes and everything, but this is the documentary evidence.'

Anna's hand shook as she took the USB from

him. 'Why am I taking this? You've got all the evidence on your laptop, right?'

'Back-up. I didn't have time to copy this to your laptop at site. Download it the minute you get back to your room,' he said. He swallowed. 'In case you're right and anything happens, and we get split up.'

'Did you email this back to our head office?'

'The connection was dreadful. I think some of it got through.' His face fell. 'But given what we know, I can't guarantee the email will reach them without being intercepted. I used the encryption key I told you about, but—'

Anna nodded. Neither of them was prepared to voice their fears. 'See you in a bit.' She tucked the USB into her jeans pocket and jogged towards the bungalow at the far end.

With a bar just off the reception area, and the tendency for the ex-pat workers to get rowdy after a day's work, she'd intentionally chosen accommodation as far away from the main building as possible.

The trees above provided some relief from the day's heat, and as she climbed the steps up to the wooden porch and wiggled her key into the door lock, she breathed a sigh of relief as the coolness from the air conditioning enveloped her.

She locked the door behind her, shot the bolt across, and dropped her backpack on the bed.

She pulled her laptop from her backpack, logged on, and plugged in the USB stick.

While the files uploaded, she eyed the bathroom longingly but realised there was no time for the luxury of a shower. She shrugged the high-visibility orange shirt off her shoulders, replaced it with a plain black t-shirt, and tied a sweatshirt round her waist. Next, she packed the remainder of her clothes, not worrying about folding anything, and threw shampoo and bottles of sunscreen into her suitcase.

It didn't take long – she and Benji were only meant to be in the country for three weeks to conclude an audit they'd started from the relative luxury of their Rotterdam offices.

Her eyes fell to the laptop screen. The download complete, she closed down the computer and put it back in her bag, then took the USB stick, placed it on the floor, and crushed it under her heel.

She collected the fragments, then hurried to the bathroom, wrapped them in toilet paper, and flushed them.

Anna thought back to the phone call she'd had with her father two hours ago. When Benji had knocked on her temporary office door and showed her the data on his laptop screen, panic had set in as she realised they'd uncovered much more than a simple hacking theft.

She'd risen from her desk and slammed the door shut, before she and Benji had had a heated conversation about what to do next. She knew that whoever had set the plan in motion had likely installed an alarm on the system that would warn of any unwanted attention, and given the level of intricacy involved, would also be able to pinpoint their exact location.

After ten minutes, Benji had agreed to her plan.

The phone lines in Western Sahara were notoriously bad, and when they couldn't get through to their office, Anna had managed to phone her father in Arizona, the relief bringing tears to her eyes when she heard his voice.

He'd agreed with her assumptions and told them to pack and leave as soon as possible. Anna's father had connections – he'd do everything he could to have someone meet them at the airport and see them to safety.

All they had to do was get to the airport at Laâyoune.

Since then, Anna had tried to phone him with updates, but her calls had gone straight to voicemail.

Anna returned to the bedroom, finished packing her suitcase, and zipped the lid shut. She smoothed out the creases in the fresh bed linen and checked the room.

None of her belongings remained in sight.

She checked her watch again. Five more minutes until she was due to meet Benji.

They'd hired a small sedan when they'd landed at the occupied country's only international airport three weeks ago, and it had remained in the mining camp's parking lot since their arrival. A sickness filled her with dread as she realised the engine might not start; she knew how temperamental vehicles could be in harsh climates and cursed her own oversight at not checking the oil and coolant levels on a regular basis.

A loud shout interrupted her thoughts, and she edged to the window, peering through the net curtains.

She stifled a scream.

A group of men were standing at the entrance to the grove that shaded the bungalows, assault rifles cradled in their hands, their camouflage fatigues leaving no doubt as to the reason for their presence. As one, they aimed at a crowd of workers who were running wide-eyed from the main camp and attempting to run between the buildings to escape the armed men.

The panicked screams and shouts of the construction workers grew louder as gunfire pierced the air, the people at the back of the crowd falling to the dirt as they were cut down behind their stumbling co-workers.

Anna's knuckles turned white as she gripped the window frame and shrank back into the shadows of the room, unable to tear her eyes away from the carnage.

As the men with the weapons grew closer, they stopped firing, and the crowd tore through the shrubs that separated the grove from the car park beyond the main entrance, disappearing from sight, the shock in their voices still audible.

Anna cursed under her breath.

The militia had worked faster than she'd given them credit for. No doubt the alarm had been raised when she and Benji had first discovered the security breach, which meant that their fears were founded and that they had been under surveillance.

She tugged the curtains closed and switched off the air conditioning, then pushed her suitcase under the bed and pulled the counterpane down until it concealed the luggage. Next, she pulled out her mobile phone, turned it onto silent and disabled the vibration option, then punched in the speed dial to her father's Arizona ranch.

She noticed the spinning ceiling fan, and killed the switch next to her shoulder while a distant dialling tone reached her ears.

She swore as it went to voicemail, and ended the call.

She almost dropped the phone as two loud gunshots reverberated through the complex.

'No,' she murmured.

She edged back towards the window, and knelt before tweaking the lower edge of the curtain to one side. She covered her mouth with her hand to stop herself from crying out as Benji's struggling form was dragged from his room by two men and dumped on the small wooden covered deck that surrounded the bungalow.

He was bleeding from a wound in his leg, screaming in agony and terror before one of the men aimed a gun at his face and pulled the trigger.

Anna whimpered, dropped the curtain back into place, and scurried across the room. As she passed her daypack on the floor next to the bed, she grabbed it, swinging it over her shoulder, and then headed for the bathroom.

She crouched on the tiled floor and hit the speed dial for her father once more. It rang three times, and her mind filled with images of the satellite phone that sat in a cradle in her father's office when he wasn't patrolling the ranch, overseeing the business of a busy operation.

She forced back tears as the ring tone died, replaced with a single, lonesome *beep,* and hung up.

Shouts from outside reached her ears, and she realised she was rapidly running out of time.

Anna tucked the phone into the side pocket of her backpack and turned her attention to the small window above the sink.

She wrapped her fingers around the metal latch and pulled.

It didn't move.

She swore under her breath, positioned herself so she was wedged against the vanity unit with her feet planted each side of the sink, and tried again, pushing her legs against the unit while she pulled with as much strength as she could muster.

She gasped as the latch gave a little under her touch, re-positioned herself, and pulled, gritting her teeth.

The latch shifted in its mounting, a small amount of dried paint spilling over the sink as the metal fastening gave way.

Anna's attention moved to the frame, a wooden

surface thickly caked in layers of paint. She placed her palms against it, and shoved.

It held firm.

She froze at a shout from below the bathroom window, and held her breath.

An order was barked, further away, and then footsteps retreated from the bungalow.

Did they hear me?

She counted to ten and then exhaled and turned her attention back to the task at hand, desperation seizing her as she realised her life depended on being able to hide – and fast.

The voices outside convinced her that any attempt to escape would be futile. She'd be located and killed, just like Benji, within seconds.

She bit back tears at the thought of the terror he must have felt as the armed men had burst into his room and tried to focus her anger and fear at the window frame under her touch.

'Come *on*,' she hissed under her breath, and pushed once more.

She forced herself to block out the terrifying sounds emanating from beyond her bungalow and instead used the heel of her hand to punch the window, inching it away from years of encrusted mould.

Terrified, she swore under her breath, and then shoved with both hands.

The window frame gave way so fast that she almost fell backwards onto the bathroom tiles. For a few precious seconds, she stood with her hands either side of the sink, breathing hard.

Another shout from outside, followed by a single gunshot, galvanised her into action.

They were searching the bungalows, one by one, killing anyone who stood in their way.

A moan escaped her lips, and her father's voice echoed in her head.

If you're ever caught up in a terrorist attack, don't try to run unless it's safe. Hide. Keep your head down. Stay quiet.

Anna swept her backpack up off the floor and tossed it onto the vanity unit before scrambling up.

She edged the window open wider and grimaced as the hinges placed along the top length of the wooden frame squeaked.

Her heartbeat thumping in her ears, she strained to hear any movement beyond the back of the bungalow.

Screams and shouting, closely followed by more gunfire, echoed across the main camp, but she saw no one emerge from behind the building.

Anna's head jerked up at the sound of a loud

crash against the front door of the bungalow, and she leapt up and pushed open the bathroom window, her dusty handprints visible up the wall.

She dived for the small opening and began to wiggle her way through, head first.

She cursed under her breath as her hip scraped the edges of the frame, and then forced herself back, trying to wiggle her way through the narrow gap. She twisted her shoulders until she could slide the top half of her body through, and then tried to twist around.

Her belt caught on the frame, the woodwork digging into her flesh.

She bit her lip, knowing that if she cried out, the armed men would find her within seconds.

She gritted her teeth and pushed again, but she couldn't get through the gap.

Defeated, she wiggled backwards until her knees met the surface of the vanity unit, and then lowered herself to the floor. She rummaged in the side pocket of her backpack and pulled out her mobile phone, leaned against the sink, and pressed the speed dial for her father's number once more.

At last, she got a signal, and then her father's voicemail message reached her ears. She took a deep breath.

'Dad? Tell Mom I'm sorry. I love you.'

THREE

Nasir Abbas hurried after the tall Englishman, his robe hitched up so he could move his feet with ease and keep pace with the man's long strides.

He muttered under his breath, a steady stream of Arabic that cursed Dan and his good luck. He'd been warned the man was a highly trained operative, but he'd seen nothing in the past two weeks he'd been observing him that suggested anything other than a typical Englishman on holiday.

The man drank beer, hung out with his neighbours in the harbour, and without fail walked to the same café and convenience store every day.

He'd lost track of the Englishman in France

several months ago, the man's boat disappearing from its moorings under cover of darkness, and it had taken several weeks of hard work and extortionate bribes to relocate him.

How he'd escaped the explosion on the boat was unprecedented.

Abbas clenched his fist as he paused several paces behind the man at a busy intersection and feigned interest in a display of kitchenware at one of the shop fronts lining the street.

He glanced over his shoulder, in time to see Dan jog across the road.

He cursed, waved away the shopkeeper that approached, mumbled something about running late, and dashed after his quarry.

He slowed as he crossed the street, taking his time, aware of the need to keep the drivers of the passing vehicles happy so they didn't sound their horns at him and draw unwanted attention.

Abbas reached the other side and stayed in the shadows, his eyes never leaving Dan's back as he turned right and into a busy marketplace.

He was easy to track, being much taller than any of the locals and most of the tourists that flocked around the stalls. It was just as well – the narrow pedestrianised street was packed with people bartering over fruit and vegetables, or browsing through the souvenirs that covered blankets and rugs laid out on the floor.

The town's streets criss-crossed each other in a style reminiscent of European urban planning, yet it was still possible to become disorientated within the labyrinth of buildings.

When he'd first arrived, Abbas had relied on the wider thoroughfares to get his bearings; if he found himself lost, he simply walked until he reached one of the wider, busier streets, then set off once more.

His planning had paid off; now, he walked the streets as confidently as a local.

He jumped at a loud call to his left as an elderly merchant pulling a handcart laden with fruit bellowed at pedestrians to let him through the throng, before a goat scampered past, a young boy yelling at it as he pushed past Abbas and disappeared from view.

Up ahead, the Englishman had stopped at one of the stalls as if to get his bearings and then darted off towards the left.

Abbas hurried to catch up, in time to see the man disappear up a narrow side street.

He hung back, seeing that the road was too narrow, with doorways opening right into the thoroughfare, and nowhere to hide if the man turned – Abbas would be too exposed.

Instead, he waited impatiently while Dan strolled unhurriedly along the street as if relishing the shade while he could. At the end of the street, a flight of stairs led up to the next street where traffic flashed past, and here he turned right.

Abbas ran as fast as he could, his sandals kicking up dust as he manoeuvred his significant bulk along the street and towards the steps. Halfway up, his heart pounding, his breathing ragged, he wondered at the irony if he should drop dead from a heart attack whilst in pursuit.

He reached the top of the steps and staggered to a halt, searching the crowded path for the Englishman. His breath escaped his lips in loud pants, and he glared at a woman who stared at him as she passed.

She quickly lowered her eyes, readjusted her headscarf around her face, and hurried away.

Abbas swallowed. If he'd lost the Englishman now, there would be little mercy from his superiors.

He almost cried out with relief as he spotted the tall man halfway down the street, his pace unwavering despite the steep climb up the steps.

Abbas pushed people out of the way as he strived to catch up, then slowed his pace once more when he was satisfied he had enough space between him and his target.

It had taken several weeks to track him down, with Abbas's superiors almost admitting defeat once the man had left England. However, they'd managed to find him, almost by accident, and Abbas had received a phone call early one evening that had galvanised him into action. He'd never doubted the hatred that his superior held for Dan Taylor, and his loyalty meant he would do everything possible to secure justice for the man he looked up to.

He frowned as the Englishman turned right and walked out in front of the traffic, trusting that the vehicles would make way for him. The man's whole body language screamed confidence, and he appeared angry.

Abbas smiled. The loss of the boat had evidently soured the man's mood, at least.

Dan slowed, checked his watch, and began to walk up the steps that led into the building that took up the whole side of the block.

Abbas moved into the shadow of an awning outside a café and pulled a mobile phone from his robe. He scowled at a teenager that passed him, the youngster dressed in Western clothing complete with a fake American university-emblazoned t-shirt, and hit the speed dial.

His call was answered within three rings.

He didn't bother with introductions. It wouldn't be appreciated by his superior at the other end of the line.

'He wasn't on the boat when the explosives detonated.'

'What went wrong?'

'He received a phone call as he entered the harbour area. It delayed his arrival back at the vessel.'

'That is unfortunate.' A pause. 'Did anyone see you?'

'No.'

'Where are you now?'

'Outside the Argan Hotel. He left the harbour and just arrived here.'

'Checking in?'

'Hard to tell. Wasn't carrying anything, but then everything he owned was on that boat.'

'Monitor the situation. Follow him if he leaves, and report back. Kill him if the opportunity arises. Our plans proceed regardless, but it would be better if Mr Taylor wasn't around to try to stop us.'

'I understand.'

Abbas ended the call and tucked the phone

away. He checked his surroundings to make sure his conversation hadn't been overheard, and then wandered along to a café under the awning, ordered a coffee, and settled at one of the tables, his eyes focused on the doors to the hotel.

He was prepared for a long wait.

FOUR

Dan gave the uniformed doorman a curt nod as he stalked across the threshold of the five-star hotel and into the coolness of the reception area.

The hotel's owners had renovated a set of four traditional three-storey houses that enclosed a tranquil courtyard, the main feature of which was a fountain set in the middle of the mosaic floor tiles. Next to it, a gnarled argan tree presided, its elderly branches providing shade during the noon hours when the sun beat overhead.

The reception desk had been positioned to the left of the front door, vine leaves sprawling from the terraces above providing an unusual but effective backdrop to the space.

Dan's boots smacked the surface of the marble-tiled floor, and he waved away the man who slipped from behind the reception desk to approach him, his smile fading under Dan's withering glare.

Dan hooked his sunglasses over the collar of his t-shirt while he gauged the layout of the hotel, and then spotted the marble staircase set into the rear corner of the space.

By the time he reached the second floor, he was beginning to wonder if he was making a mistake.

What if it was a trap? What if David was planning to have him arrested and spirited back to the UK?

And who the hell had destroyed his boat?

As the stairs ended on the third landing, he stepped into a wide corridor, its marble floor dappled with sunlight from openings carved out of the walls. The stonework lent a coolness to the space, which resonated with a quiet serenity that jarred with the heat and bustle he'd left outside.

From his position, he had a clear view of the reception desk and front door. The rest of the hotel seemed to be deserted while its tourist guests were out exploring for the day.

He checked his watch. It had taken him twenty minutes to reach the hotel, and he wondered how his life might change within the next hour. If he was going to have second thoughts, it was now or never.

The sound of a door opening behind him interrupted his thoughts, and he turned, ready to fight, and then relaxed.

'Mel.'

'Hey.'

Tall, blonde, Melissa Harper was a top-notch analyst and, if she was here with David, had added "field agent" to her extensive list of skills as well.

Dan gave her a brief hug. 'You've lost the hat and the piercings.'

A faint smile crossed her lips as she glanced down at her jeans and t-shirt. 'A compromise,' she said, and shrugged.

Dan nodded. No doubt the twenty-something was settling in well at the Energy Protection Group. 'What's going on?'

'Not here,' she said, indicating the doors to the other hotel suites. 'Too many ears. Come on.'

She led the way back towards the open door from which she'd appeared, waited for Dan to join her, and then closed it behind them.

A man turned away from the window, a little shorter than Dan, his hair showing the first flecks of grey. He held out his hand.

'Dan.'

'David.'

The head of the Energy Protection Group

gestured to a dining table that had been set up as a temporary command post. 'Shall we sit?'

Dan folded his arms across his chest. 'I'd prefer not to.'

His eyes swept the room, taking in the Moroccan style of furnishings – sofas with kilim cushions for guests to curl up on, a colourful glass tea service set out on a low square table, and bright rugs covering the stone floor.

He ignored it all and stalked across the room to the window, edged to one side, and twitched the curtain.

The building opposite housed cafés and an international fast-food chain on the lower level, the tables and chairs filled with both locals and tourists, while another hotel took up the next two levels. Dan ran a practiced eye over the windows across from his position and noted they were all sealed.

'I'm surprised you've got no-one covering your back,' said Dan.

'You're a wanted man in some circles, Taylor, not a threat.'

'Who's brilliant idea was this? Yours?'

'Like I said before, it was the general who suggested you. The Prime Minister agreed.'

'He really doesn't want me to make it back to the UK alive, does he?'

'It's not like that, Dan. He's trying to help. Despite what happened, I think he realises that what his predecessor did to you was wrong.'

'Good grief, a politician with a conscience?'

David sighed. 'Don't be sarcastic.'

Dan stared through the window down to the pavement below and watched a pair of girls, likely European tourists judging by their bare legs, walk past the hotel. 'What has all this got to do with me?'

'The current Prime Minister is the only one who holds the key to overthrowing any criminal conviction against you,' explained David. 'Everyone else has to go by the official record. He knows what you're capable of, and the circumstances that you left the country under.'

'So he's bribing me to help him?'

'Face it, Dan. He's your only chance. You didn't help matters by running.'

Dan swore. 'If I do this, can you find out who destroyed my boat?'

'You concentrate on that when you've got Anna, and she's on a plane back to the United States and her father.' He ignored the disbelieving look Dan shot him. 'I'll have a word, see if I can get someone here to start an investigation while you're away. It'll give you a head start, okay?'

Dan closed his eyes, willing himself not to curse

out loud with exasperation. David had him in a corner, and he knew it.

'Look, it'll be good PR for the Energy Protection Group, too,' David continued. 'It'll show that we can operate as Tier One contractors, rather than a section tied to the government.'

Great, thought Dan. *More black ops.*

He groaned and turned away from the bright sunlight, then blinked to adjust his eyesight to the subdued hues of the hotel room. 'Okay, you win. I'll do it,' he said.

'Excellent. I'll let the PM know.'

'I'm only doing this because it's the general's daughter, mind.'

'Right-o.'

'Guys? Can we stop the bickering?' Mel interrupted. 'There's a damsel in distress to be rescued.'

Dan turned and arched his eyebrow at her. 'I'll have you know Anna Collins is one of the best civilian sharpshooters I've seen,' he said. 'I wouldn't call her a "damsel in distress."'

'Whatever,' said Mel, and pointed at her computer screen. 'Get over here and check out this briefing information I've pulled together for you.'

Dan pulled out a chair and sat down with an exasperated sigh. He wanted to help Anna, but he wished he was dealing directly with the general, not having to take orders from David quite so soon; the way the man handed out information in a piecemeal fashion had begun to grate on his nerves last time they'd worked together, and it seemed that nothing had changed in the interim.

Mel spun her laptop screen round so Dan could see it. 'Three weeks ago, Anna Collins and her colleague, Benji van Wyk, arrived in Western Sahara and drove from the Laâyoune International Airport to this new mine development a hundred miles east of the city.'

'What's there?'

'A new phosphate mine,' said David. 'Extremely controversial, given that Morocco has awarded an American contractor a mining lease on land it illegally occupies, according to international law.'

'The mining lease was granted on the basis that the Moroccan government would use any profit to benefit the Sahrawi people that live in Moroccan-occupied Western Sahara,' added Mel. 'But if past history is any indicator, they'll probably use it to bolster their military presence in the territory instead.'

'So why were Anna and her colleague there?'

'Anna works for a forensic accounting and IT

organisation based in Rotterdam,' said David. 'She's been there since leaving university. The organisation carries out investigations into fraud and financial theft from companies all around the world.'

'I spoke with her manager,' said Mel. 'The mining contractor who's developing the phosphate mine had orders in for long-lead time equipment needed for the mining operation. Specifically, a multi-million dollar dragline that would be used to scrape the earth and rocks away from the open-cut mine face to expose the phosphate vein.'

'What happened?'

'The mining company's computer system was hacked, and unfortunately they didn't realise until it was too late,' said Mel. 'When they issued the second milestone payment for the equipment, it never arrived in the supplier's bank account.'

'That happened two months ago,' said David. 'By the time the different accounting departments in each company realised what had happened, it was too late. The mining contractor contacted their insurers and the FBI to report the theft.'

'How did Anna get involved?' said Dan.

'The mining company's insurers contracted their investigation out to Anna's employers,' said David. 'They're considered experts in their field. Anna and

Benji were tasked with following the money to try and expose where it had gone, including which financial institutions might have been used to flush the funds through. Part of their investigation was to visit the mine and interview the personnel involved, to help build a timeline and to find out how the system had been breached. Van Wyk is the technical guru; Anna manages the financial side of the investigation.'

'Why on earth did she end up on the run?'

'The General received a voicemail message from Anna earlier today, just after oh nine hundred hours local time. He picked up the message thirty minutes later. All Anna could tell him was that she was in trouble. Mel – have you got a copy of the original voicemail message?'

'Sure.' The analyst moved her mouse across the screen and selected a file, then pressed the "play" button.

Dan's breath caught in his chest at the sound of Anna's voice.

'Benji and I found something, and I think we're in trouble. A lot of trouble. I really need to talk to you, Dad.'

'Not long after that, Anna managed to get hold of her father and speak to him,' said Mel. 'He told her to get away as soon as possible and head for the airport. Later, the general received another message.'

'*Dad? Tell Mom I'm sorry. I love you.*'

'Obviously, whoever she was scared of was close by, which is why she's whispering,' said David. His eyes hardened as he watched Dan. 'The general wouldn't call us if he didn't think Anna's life was in danger.'

'Shit,' said Mel, her hand covering her mouse as she clicked through a series of windows, flicking from one to the other at speed.

'What's going on?' David moved closer, his eyebrows knitting together.

'I'm getting reports through the local police channels that the camp's been attacked by militants,' said Mel. 'They're saying there are casualties, but not how many – or whether any ex-pats are involved.'

'Shit.' Dan's heartbeat ratcheted up a notch. 'Anna wasn't kidding when she said she was in trouble, was she? What else is there?'

'By the time the staff at the camp managed to get hold of the police, the armed group that ambushed the camp was long gone.'

'Any sighting of Anna with them?'

'Negative. The staff members were all hiding

under desks and anywhere else they could after they heard the gunfire. No-one saw anything.'

Dan frowned. 'That means she either wasn't there, or they haven't found her. Nor have the police.'

'Exactly,' said Mel.

Dan's pulse quickened, his mind already creating scenarios, planning what he'd need to do the moment he arrived in Western Sahara. He turned his attention to Mel.

'How soon can you get me on a plane to Laâyoune?'

She grinned and held up a printed flight manifest. 'Plane leaves in one hour. Best pack.'

Dan glared at her. 'I'm travelling light. My clothes are at the bottom of Essaouria harbour, remember?'

Mel's grin disappeared, her face flushing before she gathered herself and reached across to a leather pouch embossed with the seal of Her Majesty's Government. She flipped it open, rummaged through the contents, and passed him a credit card.

'Best go shopping, then,' she said, keeping her tone light. 'Just remember who's picking up the bill.'

Dan snatched the flight manifest and credit card. 'My passport was on the boat.'

Mel reached into the leather pouch and withdrew a new EU passport and passed it to him.

Curious, he opened it and checked the photograph inside. 'This is an old one.'

'Good thing you age well.' She stuck her tongue out at him.

His mouth quirked. He knew he was being an asshole, but right now he didn't care.

'Anything else?'

David handed him a mobile phone. 'Satellite capability. The phone and internet reception in Western Sahara are non-existent in places. Keep us posted, and if you need help, call.' He shrugged. 'There won't be much we can do, but at least we'll know where you are.'

'Great, that's reassuring to know.'

'You're going to have to come up with a reason for your being there,' said David. 'The place will be crawling with police now, and most likely the military as well.'

'Any idea who the militants are?'

'Two possibilities,' said Mel. 'Either a contingent of Sahrawi or a possible Al Qaeda-linked cell.'

Dan cursed under his breath. 'Great. Just great. I come out of retirement and take on Al Qaeda single-handed.'

The sarcasm was lost on Mel. 'If it *is* Al Qaeda, it'll be one of the smaller groups that are rumoured to be operating in the area. You've got to bear in mind, though, that the phosphate mining is extremely controversial, so it could be a local group with no links to recognised terrorism groups.'

'Spoilt for choice, then,' Dan muttered.

FIVE

Laâyoune, Western Sahara

Dan hissed through his teeth as the afternoon sunlight bathing the tarmac under the aircraft assaulted his eyes. He pulled his sunglasses out of his new backpack and descended the steps from the fuselage.

The flight had been uneventful, a short one-hour trip from Morocco into the occupied territory that gave him time to read through the short dossier Mel had handed to him.

He'd shopped for clothes at the airport in Essaouria, buying a pair of lightweight trekking boots, a long-sleeved shirt, plain navy blue sweatshirt, clean underwear, and a pair of jeans.

Dan had declined a plastic shopping bag for his purchases and instead, to the bemusement of the girl serving him, proceeded to rip the tags from the clothes and shove them into his backpack.

He'd glanced at the jewellery store on his way to the departure gate, tempted to pick up a new dive watch and do some real damage to Her Majesty's credit card, but decided against it. If he took liberties, he was in no doubt that Mel would cancel the card – and he didn't yet know what he was facing, or what he might need to find Anna Collins and get her to safety.

Now, as he followed the other passengers across the tarmac towards the customs building, he began to run through what would be his immediate plans.

Once the customs formalities were complete and his new passport scrutinised, he was waved through the gates and entered the arrivals area. He found the car rental company kiosk with ease; there was only one, and the queue was beginning to grow as he took his place.

After thirty minutes of shuffling forward a fraction at a time, he finally reached the desk and the harassed rental company salesman, arranged and paid for a current year's model SUV, and ventured out through the front doors of the arrivals area.

The dry heat left him with a parched throat by the time he'd found his allotted vehicle, and he sat in the driver's seat with the air conditioning ratcheted up to full for five minutes before he tugged the door shut and acquainted himself with the controls.

Soon he was heading away from the airport and onto the highway that tracked south towards the mine site and the camp accommodation where Anna Collins had last been seen.

He found a truck stop ten minutes later and swung into the dusty parking area, locked the door, and entered the small store, stocking up on snacks and plenty of water before continuing his journey.

He had no idea what to expect when he arrived at the camp, or when he and Anna would be able to get a flight out of the country – if he could find her.

He tried not to think of the alternatives: that he was too late, or she had vanished without a trace.

Once clear of the city, the highway angled south and the landscape returned to a rocky, flat terrain. Dan recalled an Arabic word from his time in the Middle East – *hamada* – that described the scrubby earth and its pitiful attempts at sustaining life between the stones and boulders.

The SUV rumbled over potholes and cracks in the road, the asphalt broken up by a combination of the harsh desert temperatures and heavy construction machinery that thundered between the new mine and the capital. Here and there, dead foxes and rabbits lay to the side of the road, victims of the increased traffic.

Dan's fingers gripped the steering wheel a little tighter, and he forced himself to concentrate on the road ahead. It wouldn't do to fall asleep at the wheel and drift in front of one of the trucks that might travel from the opposite direction.

After twenty minutes, the road curved left and the setting sun over Dan's shoulder glinted off a long steel structure that stretched as far as he could see.

He realised it was the conveyor belt that transported phosphate ore from the existing Bou Craa mine site through to the port at Laâyoune, one which Mel's documentation showed the new mine owners hoped to lease to transport their own ore – for a cost.

The road arced in a sweeping curve and then followed the conveyor belt in a south-easterly direction, the steel towers of electricity pylons criss-crossing over the road, providing the power required to keep the conveyor running day and night.

By the time the lights from the gantries overhanging the Bou Craa mine appeared on the horizon, the sun had disappeared and darkness enveloped the SUV on each side of the road.

Dan had forgotten how suddenly night fell in the desert – there was no twilight, no easing into the night. He reached forward and turned off the air conditioning and buzzed down the window instead; already the temperature had dropped outside, and he knew he'd be grateful for the sweatshirt he'd bought at the airport.

He slowed as he approached a junction in the road, a signpost indicating the new mine site was a further six miles away. He flicked the indicator, turned left, and bounced the vehicle over the unsealed road that bore the brunt of the construction trucks.

He squinted as headlights appeared at a bend in the road ahead of him and another vehicle barrelled towards him at speed.

'What the hell?'

Dan swung the wheel and pulled over to the side of the road to let the other vehicle pass.

As it did so, he noted it was a police car, its liveried panel work flashing past his window in an instant. A second vehicle followed in its wake, the driver's face a mask of concentration in the reflection of the lead vehicle's taillights.

Dan swore as he realised it was a coroner's vehicle.

He pulled back onto the road and pressed the accelerator, the SUV powering along the rocky surface.

Dan fought to stop the vehicle from sliding on the loose stones and gravel and cleared the distance to the camp in a couple of minutes.

His heart sank at the sight of flashing blue lights in the car park for the accommodation, and he eased the SUV to a standstill, his breathing heavy.

Two military vehicles had been parked to one side, soldiers mulling around smoking cigarettes, their faces fatigued.

To their left, six forms lay still under sheets, while a second coroner's vehicle eased away from the car park and headed towards the highway.

Dan turned off the headlights and watched for a moment, working out the pecking order amongst the officials that milled about the site before pulling the keys from the ignition and wrapping his fingers around the door release.

'Here goes nothing,' he muttered, and stepped out into the night.

SIX

With his height and obvious Western appearance, Dan had only taken a few steps when one of the soldiers noticed him and called out.

'Who are you?'

Dan held his hands up to placate the younger man and walked towards him. 'I'm from Eastern Commercial Insurance,' he said. 'Two people are staying here – they work for us. Have you seen them? What's going on?'

The soldier's posture relaxed, although his features were pained. He gestured to where his commanding officer stood talking with a high-ranking police officer. 'You'd better talk to Captain Bassam,' he said.

Dan thanked him and strode towards the senior

officials, repeating his credentials when he introduced himself.

'Captain Amjad Bassam,' said the army officer, shaking his hand, 'and this is Farid Galal from the anti-terrorism unit.'

'What's going on?' repeated Dan. 'We have two employees staying here. I heard something about an attack on the camp?'

'Mr Taylor,' began Galal, 'I regret to inform you that one of your employees, Benji van Wyk, was killed in the attack. There were many casualties.' He gestured towards the line of bodies waiting to be taken away by the coroner. 'I am very sorry.'

'What about Anna Collins? Where is she?'

Galal shifted uncomfortably and glanced at Bassam.

'We don't know,' said the army captain. He jerked his head at his soldiers. 'We've been searching the premises since it was declared safe. We haven't found her.'

Dan swallowed. 'Do you think she was taken?'

Bassam shrugged. 'It's too early to say.'

'But if she isn't here, she could have been kidnapped, right?'

'Mr Taylor,' said Galal. 'Please, it is very early on in our investigation. The attack happened only a few hours ago. As Captain Bassam informed you, tt is too early to say.'

Dan exhaled and ran his eyes over the small crowd gathered around the camp reception building. Several workers still wore their high-visibility shirts, and all looked distraught. Many sat in small groups, while two women who appeared to be camp staff wailed as their co-workers attempted to comfort them.

'Who did this?'

Galal glanced at Bassam before speaking. 'It looks like the work of a Sahrawi militia,' he began. He shrugged. 'What can I say? It's a problem for us. There are a lot of locals who don't appreciate our funding of opportunities for people in this country and seize any chance to try to tip the balance.'

Dan nodded and kept his thoughts to himself. Although he didn't agree with the politics of the country, at least the policeman's words went some way to explain the presence of the army.

'Not Al Qaeda, then?' he asked.

Bassam shook his head. 'Not in this area,' he said. 'They usually operate further north of here, closer to the refugee camps. Easier to recruit.'

'Can I see Miss Collins's accommodation, please?' Dan said. 'If you wouldn't mind?'

'We have already checked her room several times,' said Bassam. 'She hasn't returned.'

'I appreciate that,' said Dan. 'But there are potentially confidential company documents that may be lying around. I'd like to ensure that anything that belongs to Eastern Commercial is retrieved and recorded in a safe and proper manner.'

He knew he sounded pompous and uncaring, but he had to see Anna's room for himself. He had to be sure that she wasn't still in the camp, and if she had been kidnapped, he wanted to make sure no clues had been left behind as to her current whereabouts.

Galal sighed. 'I'll go with you,' he said. 'Although I can assure you, you will find nothing.'

'Thank you.'

Dan shook Bassam's hand in parting and followed Galal across the parking area to the reception building.

He felt the eyes of the mine's employees on him as he weaved his way through the small crowd, and kept his focus on the policeman's back as they turned onto a narrow path.

Spotlights had been set up along its length, and Dan's attention was drawn to the bloodstains that spattered the path and concrete wall of the reception block.

He swallowed. It had been a number of years since he'd seen carnage like this, and he'd managed to bury some of those memories. Now, he clenched his fists and concentrated on his breathing.

The path ended, and the space opened out into a group of temporary bungalows that had been set apart by clever landscaping. It gave the accommodation an almost resort-like feel.

'This is where guests of the mine stay,' explained Galal. 'The mine workers' camp is in the other direction. A bit more basic, but...' He shrugged.

'Cost effective?' Dan suggested.

'Exactly.'

'How many guests were staying here?'

'Just Mr van Wyk and Miss Collins,' said the policeman. 'They arrived two weeks ago.' He pointed at a bungalow halfway along. 'That was Mr van Wyk's.'

Dan started towards it without waiting to be invited.

'Mr Taylor, please,' said Galal, hurrying to catch up. 'There's really no need. It's not something I would wish you to see.'

Dan reached the bottom of the steps that led up

to the bungalow and glanced over his shoulder. 'It's okay. I think I should. My company will expect a full report from me.'

He gave the policeman an apologetic smile and turned his attention back to the small building as he climbed the short flight of steps onto the wooden covered deck space.

A forensic team was working under the light of a row of bright bulbs that shone from a mobile gantry, their voices muted as they carefully recorded all the evidence.

Dan folded his arms across his chest, kept away from the body of van Wyk, and forced himself to concentrate.

A bloodstain covered most of the floor area, pooling between the bare boards and across a reed mat that had been set beside the front door. Clothes lay strewn across the floor, and the bathroom had been ransacked.

The forensic team had placed markers on the floor, where one of them was now crouched, using plastic bags to collect the spent bullet casings.

'It is a terrible tragedy,' murmured Galal. 'I am sorry for your loss.'

'Where are his things?' asked Dan.

'Things?'

'He was here on business. Mobile phone, laptop computer. Things.'

The policeman spoke in rapid Arabic to one of the forensic team, who shook his head.

'No things,' said Galal. 'Maybe he left them at the mine office?'

'Maybe,' said Dan. He moved down the steps and cast his eyes around the accommodation area. 'Which one is Miss Collins's?'

'This way.'

Two more floodlights lit the area between the bungalows, and Dan noticed Galal's men patrolling the perimeter, their weapons drawn.

'How many men do you have here?'

'About eight in total,' said Galal. He shrugged. 'It's all my department could spare.' He sighed. 'It's why we need this new mine,' he added. 'We need more funding to stop terrorist attacks like this from happening in our country.'

Dan bit his tongue. There was no point starting an argument with the man about being an occupying force. Not when he needed him on his side until he found out what had happened to Anna.

Instead he slowed his pace as the man indicated a bungalow at the end of the row, set aside from the rest.

'I think Miss Collins valued her privacy,' Galal said. 'This is hers, away from everyone else.' He indicated the empty buildings next to it. 'No-one else is staying here at the moment.'

The small building was abandoned, its position at the far end of the floodlights' reach, and as Dan moved into the shadows and up the short flight of steps to the door, he shivered.

The light in the room had been left on, fully displaying the damage that had been caused to the property.

The bed had been overturned, and a suitcase had been emptied of its contents, the clothing strewn about the floor.

Dan stepped over the threshold and made his way towards the door at the back of the room, pulled a cord to his right, and blinked as a bright light illuminated a small bathroom.

Bare shelves lined the wall under a mirror that had been smashed, remnants of glass pooling in the basin below.

Dan spun on his heel and stalked back to where Galal stood at the door, waiting.

'I'd like to call my people,' he said, extracting his mobile phone. 'Do you mind?'

'Of course not,' said Galal. 'You must.'

'Can I take a look around afterwards? It'd help

with my report,' said Dan. 'I'll stay out of the way of your people.'

The policeman looked troubled for a moment, then seemed to realise the quickest way of getting the Englishman away from the camp would be to comply.

'Please, take as long as you need,' he said eventually. 'I'll let my men know to assist you if you have any questions.'

'Thank you,' said Dan, and shook his hand. 'I won't be long.'

'I must go,' said Galal. 'It is going to be a busy night.'

He gave a curt nod and strode towards his men, who were patrolling in front of the accommodation opposite Anna's bungalow.

Dan noted where the second police patrol was and moved into the shadows before dialling Mel's number.

'It's me,' he began in a loud voice, well aware that Galal was still within earshot. 'I'm at the mine camp. It's terrible. Benji van Wyk is dead. No one knows where Anna Collins is. You'd better get Ludlow on the line. I've got no idea what to do.' He ran a hand over his short hair and made sure he wore a worried expression on his face as Galal stole a glance his way.

'Have you found her?'

'Negative,' said Dan, lowering his voice and keeping an eye on Galal as the man led his men away from the bungalows and back towards the reception area. 'There are police and army here, and no-one's seen her.'

'Shit. You think she's been kidnapped?'

'The room's been ransacked, but it looks like it's been done out of spite. The only sign of a struggle is a broken mirror in the bathroom. I'd expect more damage if she was taken forcibly.'

'That's strange.'

'What's the current situation?' David's voice cut across Mel's next question.

'A forensic team is working in van Wyk's room at the moment,' Dan said. 'Looks like they've abandoned Anna's for the time being. She doesn't seem to be a priority for them. They've got six dead bodies out front, and three coroner's vehicles have already left the scene, so I'd imagine there are casualties at the hospital in Laâyoune to deal with as well.'

'What's your plan?'

'I'm going to take a look around. There's something not right about all this, but I can't put my finger on it yet.'

'Do you think the militants are still in the area?' asked David.

'Maybe. There're police patrolling the perimeter of this part of the camp at the moment, but you know as well as I do that terrorists have a habit of hanging around in case they can cause more damage.'

'Talk about being in the wrong place at the wrong time,' said Mel. 'All Anna was meant to be doing was investigating the mine company's suppliers.'

'I'm not convinced,' said Dan. 'Van Wyk's belongings have been ransacked. He was there on business, right? So, there should've been a laptop, phone – but there's nothing there. And the police and army haven't made any suggestions why. Anna's room is the same – no sign of a computer. What sort of terrorist stops to steal a laptop?'

'What are you thinking?' asked Mel.

'This wasn't a case of wrong place, wrong time,' said Dan. 'Everyone else got shot to make it look like a random act of terrorism. This was a targeted attack. They were looking for Anna and Benji.'

SEVEN

Galal barked an order at his men and sent six of them in the direction of the guest accommodation.

When Galal had returned moments before without the Englishman in tow, Amjad Bassam had been furious.

'He could be working for the media,' he growled.

The policeman had shaken his head. 'No, he was asking the wrong sorts of questions,' he argued. 'And he's not a decision-maker. He had to make a phone call to his superiors before I left him. He is of no harm to us.'

The army captain had dropped the conversation and had returned to his own team as they worked through the crowd interviewing witnesses.

Galal scratched absently at a mosquito bite on his forearm while his mind churned.

The woman disappearing was unexpected – and a concern. It hadn't been part of the original plan, and now that her colleague was dead, there was no way of telling where she was.

The camp staff had confirmed both had arrived at the same time, and his men had already interviewed the driver who had dropped them off after their hurried exit from the mining company's offices earlier that day.

Anna Collins had certainly been at the camp at some point since her departure from the mine. The only question was, where was she now?

He had sent his men to patrol the bungalows, aware that if he kept asking Taylor questions he could have aroused the man's suspicions about what had really happened at the mine camp, choosing instead to give the man some space in the hope he'd find out where the woman might be.

Surely, she'd have phoned her colleagues to tell them she was safe if she had escaped?

Once he was alone, Galal pulled out a mobile phone, one that hadn't been issued to him by the department, and dialled a number he knew by heart.

'It's me,' he said by way of introduction. 'We might have a problem. The woman evaded the attackers, and there's an Englishman who turned up. He says he's from the insurance company the woman was working for. He's been asking questions.'

He listened to the man at the other end of the call, his brow furrowing as he struggled to understand the thick accent.

'I have my men undertaking a perimeter patrol,' he said. 'They'll keep an eye on him.'

He fell silent and paced the ground next to the army truck. 'I understand,' he said. 'And if Miss Collins reappears, I'll ensure that the matter is taken care of. Permanently.'

Galal ended the call and cursed.

He thought he'd been careful to hide his gambling debts, always making sure that no-one within the police force would discover his weakness.

Now, he wished he'd never been coerced into joining the syndicate.

The gambling had alleviated the monotony for a while, before the men who played cards every week began to chip away at his resolve and use his weakness to their advantage

First, they'd played to his ego, softening him up, telling him of the rewards that awaited him if he joined their venture.

Then, his gambling debts had been allowed to increase, until the night he stood up from his place at the table and announced he wanted out.

The leader's eyes had hardened, and Galal had been pushed back into his seat, terrified, while the man set out his plans in detail: a plan that held Galal at its centre, and which would almost certainly end in Galal's death if he tried to abscond.

Galal exhaled and tapped the phone against his chin as he tried to concentrate.

Something about the man who introduced himself as Dan Taylor made him nervous.

Very nervous.

EIGHT

Dan ended his call and tucked his phone back in his pocket, then waited until the police patrol passed where he stood.

He jogged back up the stairs to Anna's room and stood on the threshold, careful not to touch anything and leave his fingerprints behind.

His gaze travelled across the clothes strewn over the floor as he tried to imagine the attackers carrying out the same exercise as they had with van Wyk's room – smashing down the door, shooting the occupant, and then ransacking the contents of the bungalow.

Except when they reached Anna's room, there was no-one there.

His eyes wandered over the bed, and then his heart lurched. In the wall above the bed, a bullet had cut deep into the plasterwork.

Dan climbed onto the bed, ducked under the immobile ceiling fan, and peered at the damage to the wall.

He glanced over his shoulder at the open door. Voices filtered on the night breeze from van Wyk's room, and Dan figured it would be at least another hour before the forensic team made their way to Anna's.

He turned his attention to the floor of the ransacked room, his eyes searching left and right until he saw what he was looking for.

From the contents of Anna's luggage that had been tossed across the floorboards he picked up a ballpoint pen and climbed back onto the bed. He removed the refill from the pen, tucked the outer casing between his teeth, and inserted the slender refill into the hole in the wall, wiggling it from side to side.

The bullet remained stubbornly stuck in the hole, and Dan cursed under his breath as sweat began to trickle down his forehead.

'Come on,' he muttered, his teeth clamping the pen in frustration.

He tried a different angle, wedging the refill above the bullet and dragging it across the brass surface until it caught.

Dan paused, caught his breath, and then gently pulled the bullet towards him. When the end of it emerged from the hole, he replaced the refill in the pen, ensured it was safely tucked into his pocket alongside his phone, and then pulled up his t-shirt and covered his fingers with the material before pulling the bullet from the wall and shoving it into a separate pocket.

He wiped the sweat from his brow and stepped down off the bed, then paused to gauge the scenario once more.

From the trajectory of the bullet, he reckoned the man who had fired the gun had shot into the room upon leaving, from frustration. The bullet had wedged too high to have any accuracy at killing the room's occupant, and there were no other bullet holes in the bungalow.

He frowned.

The attacks on the two rooms seemed clinical, with little wastage of ammunition. From his experience, terrorists didn't worry about using up bullets – their raison d'être was to cause as much mayhem, death, and destruction as possible. The whole shock factor was the reason terrorists did what they did.

Outside, nearer the reception area, the attack had been more indiscriminate. The scene of crime struck Dan as being carried out by two different teams – one tasked with hunting down Anna and her colleague, the other to create a diversion and leave behind a trail of destruction that masked the true nature of the attack on the camp.

Dan scratched his jaw as he slowly turned in the middle of the room and tried to put himself in Anna's shoes.

She would have heard the gunfire, shouting, and screaming from the reception area before hearing the shots that killed her colleague, but the bungalow left her with nowhere to hide.

He wandered into the bathroom and stared at his reflection in the shattered mirror, shards covering the vanity unit from where one of the attackers had no doubt smashed the glass with the butt of a rifle in frustration.

The window bumped in its frame above the sink, and he jumped before chastising himself. He turned to go back into the bedroom, and a thought struck him.

He spun round and pushed against the window.

It swung freely on two hinges along the top of it, providing a gap that was too small for his wide shoulders to fit through.

A petite American, on the other hand—

Dan hurried through the bungalow, slowing as he reached the door, and began walking down the steps.

The police patrol was passing in front of the bungalow, bored expressions on their faces, and he waited until they had gone before he slipped behind the building.

He made his way through the scrubby undergrowth, cursed when he caught his foot on a pipe that led from a water reservoir to the back of the building, and stopped directly under the bathroom window.

He pulled out his phone and, after checking the patrol wasn't in sight, angled the light from it onto the ground at his feet.

Nothing.

He frowned, took stock of the patrol's progress, and once satisfied he wasn't going to be disturbed, waved the light left and right across the sparse dirt.

The only footprints by the window were those of a man, the soles of the footwear leaving faint tracks in the soil similar to the size of Dan's own boots.

Dan switched off the light and stared at the open window. There were no scrape marks, no scraps of torn clothing on the latch. Then it hit him.

'You clever girl,' he murmured.

It would have been one hell of a risk, but the only chance Anna would have had to escape the attack.

Dan jogged back down the side of the bungalow, his body hugged close to the wall, and peered around the front porch.

Beams of light from the police patrol's flashlights peppered the furthest edge of the grove.

He hurried up the steps to the bungalow and re-entered the building.

Dan pushed the door closed and moved further into the room. He checked inside the wardrobe, placing his hands against the back panelling, then stopped and listened.

He knew he was on the right track; he could sense that someone else was close but simply couldn't fathom where they might be.

He stood and raised his gaze to the ceiling, but it was bare except for a light bulb and a ceiling fan.

Nowhere to hide.

He wandered into the bathroom.

He stayed still, willing his heartbeat to slow so

that it didn't pound quite so hard in his ears, and called out quietly.

'Anna? Anna, it's Dan Taylor.'

He turned in an arc, his eyes seeking out the walls, the floorboards that looked as if they hadn't been disturbed in decades. Nothing moved.

'Anna? It's safe now. They've gone.' He exhaled, beginning to doubt his own hunch.

His head jerked up at the sound of a scratching noise. 'Anna? It's okay. I'm here to take you home.'

He heard it then – a muffled sob, and then the scratching became louder, from within the bathroom.

Dan moved closer, his brow creasing.

A metallic scraping sound began next, and he realised it was coming from a large vent behind the bathroom door.

He crouched down and nearly lost his balance as the metal grille covering the vent fell away from the wall and a pale hand snaked out towards him.

'Dan?'

He knelt until he could peer into the cavity.

Anna's eyes held all the terror she had experienced over the past few hours, her breathing shallow.

'Come here,' he said. 'I've got you.'

He reached out and took her hand while she

wiggled from the space. She sat on the floor next to him, tears streaming down her cheeks.

He enveloped her in his arms as she buried her face in his chest. 'It's okay. I've got you,' he murmured. 'It's okay.'

Anna sniffed and wiped at her eyes. 'They killed Benji.'

'I know.'

She gazed up at him, and then placed her hand on his cheek. 'Dad got my message?'

Dan nodded. 'Yeah. He couldn't make it, so he sent me.' He smiled. 'So, you see, I *had* to find you. I was too scared to go back empty-handed.'

She managed a faint smile before a sob broke through her bravado.

Dan glanced over his shoulder. 'Shh,' he said, and smoothed her hair. 'The attackers have gone, but there are still local police and army outside,' he explained. 'And I don't trust them, so we need to be quiet, okay?'

'Okay.' She sniffed loudly and wiped at her eyes. 'What do we do?'

'I've got a car outside the reception area. We'll track round the perimeter behind one of the patrols to get to it. I want to make sure we get away from here without any fuss, understand?'

She nodded, and then pulled away from him.

'Wait.' She shuffled across to the open vent, reached inside, and pulled out a backpack. 'I need to take this.'

'Okay. Let's go.'

NINE

Dan checked the patrol was out of sight before wrenching the door open and leading Anna down the stairs and round the back of the building.

'Keep close, and stay quiet,' he whispered.

Anna nodded and gave him a thumbs up, and not for the first time he was grateful the general hadn't shied away from teaching his daughter basic field craft.

In fact, the general had confided in him once that he'd treated it like a game ever since Anna was old enough to walk, showing her how to move silently, how to blend in with her surroundings, and how to keep calm in a crisis.

Dan had certainly been impressed at the young

woman's quick thinking at going to ground once she'd realised fleeing from the camp and raising the alarm wasn't an option. Too many people were killed in terrorist attacks because instead of running away or hiding, they tried to find out what was going on, as if the reality of the situation was too grave to comprehend.

Now, Dan crept along the back of the bungalow, his hand around Anna's, guiding her through the gloom.

As they approached the gap separating it from the next building, the floodlights shone through and onto the high mesh fence that encircled the rear of the mining camp.

He peered closer and momentarily debated trying to climb over, before dismissing the plan when he saw a sign along the top warning of an electrical current running through it.

He suspected the military or police would have severed the power to it upon arriving at the scene, but he wasn't prepared to test his theory.

Instead, he checked the time, waited until the patrol walked in front of the bungalows, then set his stopwatch and pulled Anna across the gap with him.

He squeezed Anna's hand and held up three fingers.

Three more bungalows to go.

She nodded, her eyes wide, and as the moon scuttled out from behind a cloud, he noticed how pale her face had become.

He realised the sooner he got her to the SUV and on the way to the airport, the sooner he could ensure she wasn't going to suffer from delayed shock.

They crossed behind the building without incident, Dan checking his stopwatch and ensuring the patrol wouldn't appear at their rear before he managed to spirit Anna away.

They ran to the next building, Anna's breathing now coming in gulps, and edged along the perimeter once more.

Dan glanced over his shoulder.

The patrol was still nowhere to be seen, but they'd complete their circuit soon. He had to keep Anna moving.

He gave her arm a gentle tug and pulled her with him to the side of the building, then froze and swore under his breath.

'What is it?' Anna hissed.

'Hang on,' he murmured.

He watched in silence as the forensic team milled about on the front porch of Benji's balcony, keeping his arm outstretched to prevent Anna from pushing past him.

Muffled voices reached his ears, the sound of someone issuing instructions. There was a scraping sound as something heavy was dragged across the floor of the bungalow, then a groan as if a weight had been lifted.

'Dan? What's going on?'

Dan took a step back, retreating further into the shadows as a covered stretcher was lifted down the steps of the bungalow. He wheeled round and pulled Anna to him.

'They're moving Benji,' he whispered. 'Don't look.'

Anna bit back a sob as she buried her face in his chest, her hands gripping his arms as she fought to control her emotions.

He ran his hands over her back, her body trembling with fright as he tried to soothe her. He lifted his gaze to the direction from which they'd escaped, and his heart lurched.

'They're coming,' he said, and gently pushed her away. 'There'll be time to mourn Benji properly later,' he added. 'But we have to go now.'

He didn't wait for her answer. He grasped her hand and pulled her across the gap.

He glimpsed a small gathering of police and

military personnel gawping at Benji's body as it was carried away, before he and Anna plunged back into the shadows behind the building.

An idea began to form in his mind, and he quickened his pace.

At the far end of the bungalow, he finally saw the brick wall of the reception building in front of him and bent down to Anna.

'I need you to be brave,' he said. 'They're going to bring Benji past us, but we need to use him as a distraction to get you away from here, understand?'

He saw her swallow, her eyes wide, and then she nodded.

'I know this isn't going to be easy for you,' he said, and squeezed her hand. 'But it's our only chance.'

'Okay,' she whispered, her voice shaking. 'Just get me out of here.'

He clenched his jaw and turned his attention back to the reception block. The path was deserted for the moment, but as the stretcher-bearers moved past with Benji's body laid out between them, the remainder of the forensic team and the military personnel that had been hanging around the front of the bungalow followed, no doubt taking advantage of a brief respite from the evening's proceedings before returning to their tasks.

Dan peered over his shoulder, craning his neck until he could see along the gradual curve of the perimeter fence and checked the patrol's progress.

They had reached Anna's bungalow and had stopped, the beams from their flashlights bouncing off the external walls.

Anna tapped him on the arm. 'They're going.'

He turned back to the stretcher-bearers and their rag-tag followers. Sure enough, the small party had reached the path that wound through the reception area and out to the parking lot, their voices louder, one even laughing as they left the carnage of the bungalow behind them.

'Let's go,' said Dan.

He jogged along the side of the bungalow, checked there were no stragglers, and then ran across the bare expanse towards the path.

The tall shrubs separating it from the car park had only been installed for decoration rather than any attempt at a boundary line, and he was able to push through the foliage with Anna in tow with ease, dropping into a crouch and pulling her down beside him.

He pulled a branch to one side and checked his bearings, and exhaled with relief.

The SUV sat only a few metres away, and he

and Anna had emerged along the blind side of one of the army trucks.

He crawled through the last of the undergrowth, beckoned to Anna, and then led her quickly towards the car. They dropped into a crouch beside the back door, hidden from view, and Dan reached in his pocket for the key fob and then swore.

'What is it?' Anna hissed.

'It's locked.'

'But you have the key.'

'Yeah, but they'll see the lights flash when I unlock it.'

'Shit.'

'You're definitely the general's daughter.'

She ignored the remark. 'What are we going to do?'

Dan held up his hand and straightened so he could see through the windows to the camp entrance. Emergency workers still sat with small groups of survivors while Galal's men took statements, but they all stopped and turned to look as the stretcher-bearers rounded the corner of the reception area.

A woman began to wail at the sight of another dead body, and the other people's voices soon grew louder, some demanding from the army that they stop smoking their cigarettes and find the attackers.

The stretcher-bearers struggled with the weight of the gurney as the small mob grew around them, until the forensic team shouted over the cacophony and tried to calm the panicked survivors.

A thin smile crossed Dan's lips, and he hit the key fob.

The doors to the SUV unlocked with a dull *clunk*, and the indicator lights flashed once.

Dan froze, watching the crowd.

He waited, letting the crowd move away from the stretcher, and stayed still until he was absolutely sure no-one had seen the car lights.

'Okay, now,' he said, and beckoned to Anna.

He swung open the back door enough to let her squeeze through.

'Keep your head down,' he commanded. 'Get yourself down in the foot well and stay still. Don't move, don't talk, until I tell you it's safe to do so.'

He waited until she'd settled and then closed the door before walking round to the driver's side. As his hand covered the door handle, he heard his name called, and turned.

Galal was hurrying towards him.

'Mr Taylor? Where are you going?'

Dan pulled out his mobile phone and held it up.

'My office called. They want me to return to Laâyoune and provide updates from my hotel there.' He frowned. 'You're sure you have absolutely no idea where Anna Collins is?'

The policeman shook his head. 'My guards will continue to patrol the perimeter,' he said, and gestured towards the desert beyond the mining camp. 'But as you can imagine, it will be near impossible to search the wider area until first light.'

'Can I call you for updates?' asked Dan. 'Obviously I'd like to be kept informed of developments. I'll need to let our embassy know about Ms Collins's disappearance too, if you haven't already?'

'Ah, no, in all the chaos here, we haven't had a chance to contact the embassy yet,' said Galal, his face contrite.

'Perhaps I can do that in the first instance and let them know you'll be in touch as soon as possible?'

Relief passed over the policeman's face, and he pulled out a creased business card from his tunic pocket. 'My office number is on there.'

Dan took it from him and opened the door to the SUV. 'I've got a feeling I'm going to be in for a long night,' he said, faking a yawn. 'I'll be in touch.'

The policeman nodded and raised his hand as

Dan manoeuvred the vehicle away from the army trucks and turned onto the road.

His heartbeat didn't slow until he hit the pockmarked tarmac of the main highway towards Laâyoune and pushed the accelerator to the floor.

TEN

They'd travelled twenty minutes when Dan heard movement over his shoulder and Anna grabbed the back of his seat.

'Dan? Pull over!'

He could guess what was going to happen next.

He gripped the wheel and swerved the car to the right of the road, braking swiftly and controlling the skid over the rugged terrain, the SUV slewing to an abrupt standstill.

Anna scrambled from the car, and before he could unclip his seatbelt, he heard the unmistakable sound of retching.

He switched off the headlights and gave her a few moments' privacy before he grabbed one of the bottles of water he'd stashed in the middle console and stepped out into the night air.

A cool breeze tickled the back of his neck as his boots crunched over the small stones and gravel that peppered the roadside where Anna stood doubled over, her hands on her knees.

Dan crossed the space between them in three long paces and rested his hand on her back while she finished.

'Here,' he said when she was done. 'Drink this. You know what to do. Small sips, that's all.'

'Thanks,' she managed. She took the bottle of water from him and straightened before taking a mouthful, rinsing her mouth and spitting it out onto the dirt before taking a smaller sip. 'Sorry.'

Dan shook his head, reached out, and grasped her shoulder. 'Don't apologise. I'm surprised you lasted as long as you did.'

'Me too.' Anna took another sip and pushed a stray strand of hair from her eyes.

Dan squeezed her shoulder.

In the light from the moon, he could see how pale her face was, and he vowed to keep a close eye on her until she boarded her plane back to the United States, back to her father.

In the meantime, he'd do everything in his power to protect her.

'Okay, listen,' he said. 'This is what's going to happen. When we get back in the car, I'm driving straight to Laâyoune airport. There are flights out of the country every half hour. It doesn't matter whether you fly to the Canary Islands, mainland Spain – wherever.'

Anna blinked, then ran her tongue over her lips. 'What about you?'

'I'll be there with you, one hundred per cent of the way. Right until you land back in the US and your Dad is there to meet you.'

Her eyes fell. 'Dan? I don't have my passport. It was in my other bag.'

He shrugged. 'Doesn't matter. Either your Dad or my lot will sort out a diplomatic passport. You're going home.'

Anna managed a faint smile between the tears that rolled down her cheeks. 'Thank you,' she murmured.

Dan held his hands up. 'All part of the service, ma'am.' He gestured to the half-empty water bottle. 'Finish that. Slowly, mind.'

Anna uncapped the bottle and raised it to her lips.

Whilst she drank, Dan used the light from his mobile phone to inspect the car and ensure the hurried exit off the road hadn't punctured the tyres.

Although all-wheel drive, the vehicle wasn't designed to be driven over rough terrain; it was more a fashion statement.

Dan ran his hand over the hood as he returned to where Anna stood finishing the last of the water, and stopped dead.

Anna's chin jerked up. 'What?'

Dan's eyes narrowed. 'We're going to have company,' he said, and pointed.

In the distance, far back where the track leading to the mine development lay, a pair of headlights hastened towards the main road.

'What on earth did you do?' Dan murmured.

Anna sniffed and clutched the plastic bottle between her hands. 'It started off as just another money laundering investigation,' she said. 'One of the mine's suppliers didn't get paid – the mine developer sent the money, all five point four million of it – but it never arrived in the supplier's bank account.'

'Do you know who took it?'

Anna nodded, and Dan exhaled, her gesture confirming the hunch he'd had about the attack on the mine camp.

'Get in the car,' he said. 'Now.'

Anna did as she was told, hurrying to the vehicle and then scrambling into the passenger seat while Dan ripped open the driver's door and launched himself behind the wheel.

The engine roared to life as soon as he twisted the key in the ignition.

He turned the headlights onto a low beam, enough to see the road by, and pressed the accelerator.

The SUV shot forwards, gravel and stones spitting out from under the tyres as he shifted gear and steered the vehicle onto the asphalt.

As soon as he felt the road surface under the wheels, he increased his speed.

'Do you think it's the people who killed Benji?' said Anna, her right hand wrapped around the strap that hung above her door.

'Maybe,' said Dan. 'Or it's Galal and his army pal. Maybe they've found out I don't work for the insurance company. Either way, I don't think it's a good idea to hang around and find out, do you?'

Anna remained silent, her eyes fixed on the road ahead as the desert passed by in a blur.

Dan's eyes flickered to the rear view mirror. The other vehicle's headlights were mere pinpricks in the distance, but it was maintaining its speed as it barrelled towards them as the driver tried to narrow the gap.

Anna twisted in her seat and peered out the back window.

'They're still a couple of miles away,' she said. 'What are we going to do?'

Dan steered the SUV through the wide curve in the road that bore them northwards, the conveyor belt still rumbling to their left as it worked through the night delivering ore to the port.

He flexed his fingers on the wheel. 'In the foot well, under my seat. Lean down and run your fingers across the carpet until you find a cut.'

Anna grabbed her seatbelt and unclipped it before leaning over and reaching under Dan's legs.

He checked his mirrors again.

The vehicle behind them had gained slightly, and he cursed the pathetic attempts of the SUV's small engine to increase its speed.

Anna's head knocked against his thigh.

'Sorry,' she said. 'Can't find it.'

'Further back,' he said, and tried to ignore the blonde hair splashed across his leg. Instead, he kept his eyes on the road, hoping that one of the errant goats that populated the arid region didn't suddenly decide to walk out in front of the vehicle.

'Got it.'

'Good,' he said with relief. 'Run your fingers under the cut. You'll find a—'

'Glock 19,' said Anna, and straightened, a faint smile on her lips. 'You came prepared, I see.'

'You never know.'

'I thought a Sig was your weapon of choice?'

'I'd prefer not to have to worry about a weapon at all,' said Dan, and then shrugged. 'But, you know. Bad people.'

'Where's the Sig?'

'I couldn't cross the border with it,' explained Dan. 'David arranged for that to be in the car when I picked it up from the airport.'

'How did he...?'

Dan shook his head. 'I don't know. I don't ask.'

He swore under his breath. He hadn't had a chance to check the weapon; he'd have to take his chances if it came to using it to make sure Anna got out of the country safely. He hoped to hell David had used a reputable contact to source the gun – there was no way of knowing until he fired it.

A faint *click* from the passenger seat caught his attention, and his eyes darted from the road to see what Anna was doing.

She'd begun to inspect the Glock, dropping the magazine out and pulling back the slide to check inside the open chamber. Once satisfied, she pushed the magazine back into place with the palm of her hand, and pulled back the slide to chamber the first round.

She noticed him watching and held out the weapon to him.

His mouth twitched. 'Tell you what. Why don't you hold onto that for now, and I'll tell you if you need to use it?'

'Okay.' Anna peered over her shoulder. 'They're getting closer.'

'I know.'

'What do we do?'

'Keep going. Get to the airport. I'm working on the assumption they won't try anything in a crowded place.'

Anna bit her lip and shuffled in her seat to face him, balancing her hand on the dashboard as Dan steered around a large pothole in the asphalt.

'In case I don't get the chance to tell you later, thank you for coming to find me.'

'Hey, it might not be that bad – it could just be one of the emergency vehicles trying to get back to the city as well.'

'But you don't believe that.'

Dan exhaled. There would be no convincing the woman sitting next to him, so he figured honesty was the best policy. 'No. No, I don't. I think whatever you uncovered at the mining project has some very powerful people very worried.'

'Yeah. Me too.'

Dan rolled his shoulders, and then his heart lurched.

Up ahead, about a mile away, he could see the flashing blue and red lights of emergency vehicles.

The highway had straightened out as it drew closer to the city, and he noticed the tell-tale sign of brake lights flaring in the distance as a vehicle slowed ahead of them.

Dan slowed, his heartbeat racing as he checked the rear view mirror.

Their pursuer was still behind them, doggedly keeping pace.

A trickle of sweat began at his forehead, and his fingers gripped the steering wheel harder. 'Looks like trouble.'

Anna frowned. 'Road accident?'

'No,' said Dan, his jaw clenched. 'Road *block*.'

ELEVEN

The sight of the emergency lights up ahead broke Anna's resolve, and she began to sob quietly.

'We're never going to get out of here alive,' she whispered.

Dan ignored her; he was trying to recall what he'd seen on either side of the road when he'd driven to the mine camp earlier.

A flat landscape stretched for miles, broken up by scrubby bushes, rocks, and the occasional boulder.

Dan hoped the boulders were extremely occasional – the SUV simply wasn't designed for roughing it, and he couldn't risk ripping the suspension from the chassis if his plan was going to work.

A stone structure loomed in the distance, and he remembered a series of small dwellings that had been set back from the road, the tiny houses built from stone with chickens and goats milling about.

It would have to do.

He switched off the lights, waited a few seconds, and then swerved the vehicle over to the right, bumping over the verge and into the scrub. He pushed his foot to the floor, ignoring Anna's cry as the SUV lurched over the terrain, jostling them in their seats.

'Hold on.' He gritted his teeth, powered the vehicle past the first building, and then slew it to a halt behind the next.

He reached out, turned off the engine, then opened his door and stepped onto the running board, leaning on the roof of the vehicle as his eyes swept the road.

The pursuit vehicle shot past before slowing as it reached the short queue at the roadblock. Its brake lights flared, and then the driver began a three-point turn in the middle of the road until the vehicle faced back the way it had come.

It remained at a standstill.

Dan's eyes followed the line of traffic past the road block.

Three police cars had formed a cordon blocking

the lane into the city, whereas the sparse traffic leaving the area was free to move. One of the police cars was parked on the side of the road, evidently as backup to the officers who were manning the blockade. All were armed.

Dan bent down and peered into the SUV, Anna's eyes wide as she leaned across.

'What's going on?'

'We're not out of trouble yet,' he said. He pointed at the glove compartment in front of her. 'In there. Binoculars. Pass them up.'

He raised his gaze back to the blockade, his mind working. He heard the clatter of the lid to the glove compartment opening, and then Anna called up to him.

'Here.'

'Thanks.'

He raised the binoculars and tweaked the focus until he had a clear view of the blockade.

There were six armed police in total, plus he presumed two more men in the vehicle that had followed them away from the mining camp. He wondered if Galal was in attendance but couldn't make out the occupants of the vehicle in the poor light.

He tipped the binoculars back towards the men managing the roadblock and frowned.

All wore the uniform of the Moroccan police, yet the weapons they carried were wrong.

They brandished what looked like Russian 9mm pistols and rifles, not the American- and German-built and supplied weaponry normally carried by Moroccan forces.

'Something stinks about this,' he muttered.

He swept the binoculars across the landscape, following the line of traffic beyond the roadblock and then starting again, this time from his own side of the roadblock.

As his eyes scanned the moonlit terrain, something caught his eye.

He tracked back along his line of vision and then refocused the binoculars and swore loudly.

A fourth police car sat abandoned some way from where the road passed through the barricade. Except that its sides were riddled with bullet holes.

Dan lowered the binoculars and cursed.

He lowered himself back into the vehicle and passed the binoculars to Anna.

'What is it?' she asked. 'What's wrong?'

Dan didn't answer straight away. Instead, he rubbed at the stubble on his chin and stared through the windscreen, trying to put together what he'd learned so far. Eventually, he leaned back in his seat and turned to Anna.

'Who was stealing the money from the project?'

Her brow furrowed. 'We traced the initial theft to a company in Lithuania,' she said. 'But it didn't end there. We were starting to follow the money as it got split up and passed on.'

'Where did it end up?'

'A Russian-owned conglomerate in Moscow. Privately owned. Why?'

Dan ran his hand over his face, the pieces of the jigsaw falling into place.

'The men patrolling the roadblock are armed with Russian weapons,' he said. 'The Moroccan police are supplied by the United States. There are three police cars manning the blockade. A fourth is parked out in the scrub, full of bullet holes.'

Anna's eyes opened wide. 'They're not real police?'

Dan shrugged. 'I think the real police are dead. If those guys are police, they're freelancing tonight.'

Anna visibly shrank in her seat. 'There's something else you should know.'

'What?'

'The money held by the Russian conglomerate only stayed in its account for a few days. After that, it started to get re-distributed – back to Morocco in some cases, but in smaller amounts – maybe six figures at a time – to Swiss numbered accounts. One in particular got our attention.'

'Why?'

'It's been linked to a black market arms trafficker.'

Dan swallowed. 'This gets better by the minute,' he muttered.

Anna shrugged. 'Look, it's just a hunch.'

Dan coughed out a laugh. 'Would that be the same hunch that got your colleague killed, and currently means your life is in danger?'

Anna looked down at her hands. 'Yeah. I suppose so.'

'I think you're right,' said Dan. 'I'm presuming there's more to this story.'

She nodded.

'Okay,' said Dan. 'Let's get as far away from that roadblock as we can and try to find a back way into the city by cutting cross-country. We still need to try to get to the airport.' He reached out. 'Give me the gun.'

He took the Glock from her, then walked round the back of the vehicle, bent down, and used the butt of the gun to smash each of the brake lights on the SUV. Satisfied their progress wouldn't be spotted by the men guarding the roadblock, he jogged back round to the driver's side and handed the gun back to Anna.

'Now what?'

Dan reached into his jeans pocket and pulled out his mobile phone. 'Hit the speed dial on that,' he said, turning the key in the ignition and keeping the revs low. 'I have a feeling David Ludlow is going to want to hear all about your investigation.'

TWELVE

Dan gritted his teeth and steered the SUV around a decrepit stone wall as the dialling tone to David's base in Essaouria rang loudly through the mobile phone's speakers.

He kept the vehicle at crawling pace, guessing that the police – or whoever they were – would be listening for a car travelling at speed.

Anna held the phone between them so they could both join in the conversation.

After three rings, David's voice filled the car.

'Have you got her?'

'Yes. Anna's here with me.'

'Are you okay?'

'I'm okay,' said Anna, and then cleared her throat. 'Yes, I'm okay.'

'Anna's colleague was killed by the attackers,' said Dan. 'It sounds like Anna uncovered information during a money laundering investigation that suggests that this was more than a simple financial theft.'

Static spat through the space of the car, and Dan reached out to turn down the volume. 'Say that again, David? We've got a crap signal.'

'Where are you right now?'

'We're trying to get to the airport, but there's a road block on the highway into Laâyoune,' said Dan. 'Is Mel with you?'

'Hang on.'

They waited while David turned on the speaker phone at his end, and Mel's voice crossed the broken airwaves.

'What's up?'

'Can you tap into the Laâyoune police network and find out if there's an authorised roadblock on the highway heading towards Bou Craa?' said Dan.

'Hang on.'

While the sound of Mel's fingers tapping on a keyboard reached them, David pressed on. 'What's going on, Anna? What sort of information did you find?'

'The drop in oil prices has got every oil-producing country in the world worried,' said

Anna. 'They haven't got the control they used to have over other countries by limiting supply. Even Saudi Arabia is struggling – their budget deficit this year is astronomical. However, we've seen an increase in weapons sales – old grudges are starting to show up at the economic level, not just geo-politically.' She cleared her throat. 'At the present time, there are several countries ignoring UN resolutions regarding Morocco's use of Western Sahara mineral assets.' She sighed. 'At the end of the day, there's a huge world population to feed, and you need fertilisers to provide food on such a massive scale. Hence why Morocco exports phosphate ore in large quantities to many Western countries – much against the wishes of the Sahrawi people.'

'David? Anna mentioned she believes the money was stolen by a Russian organisation. The police manning the roadblock were carrying Russian weapons. That plus a police car off to one side with bullet holes down one side makes me think either the police are corrupt—'

'Or were intercepted on the way to the call-out, killed, and this bunch of mercenaries have taken their place,' said David. 'Anna – anything else you can give us to work on?'

Anna's brow creased for a moment. 'Yes,' she

said, excitement filling her voice. 'There is. Mineral processing accounts for something like eighty-five per cent of the GDP for this area, and Morocco takes all of that. None of it goes back into local infrastructure – it finances Moroccan police and military interests in Western Sahara instead.' She sighed. 'I think someone is putting together a mercenary force here in occupied Western Sahara.'

'To take back the territory you mean?'

'Yes,' she said. 'But not in the best interests of the Sahrawi people,' she added. 'I think someone wants those mining rights for themselves.' Excitement filled her voice. 'The owners of the Russian conglomerate had a huge stake in oil for a while, but looking at the official accounts we could find, the company has been losing a significant amount of money for more than eighteen months. Look, this is just an idea—'

'Which means she's probably right,' said Dan.

Anna glared at him before continuing. 'But what if they were deliberating arming a mercenary force in Western Sahara? Not to fight a war per se, but to *start* a war?'

'Motive?' said David.

Anna thought for a second. 'Russia doesn't have a stake in the mining industry here in Western Sahara,' she said. 'Politically, it aligns itself with the

Algerian-backed Polisario, who in turn want independence returned to the region. So, Russia wouldn't openly take on Morocco – it'd be picking a fight with America, Australia, the UK, and everyone else that imports the ore they're extracting. It's too risky.'

'But if they *influenced* the locals into starting an uprising, they might cause a big enough fight that would swing the odds in Russia's favour,' said Dan. 'Wow.'

'You wouldn't need many mercenaries to do it, either,' said David. 'Just a few here and there to create dissent amongst the locals, then stand back and watch it unfold.'

'Jesus.' Dan sat for a moment, stunned as Anna and David's words sunk in. 'David, this information is dangerous,' he said. 'The sooner I can get Anna out of the country and to safety, the better.'

'Anna? Can you use the satellite feed from Dan's phone to upload the information you have, so we can —'

A loud hiss of static interrupted David's words.

Dan waited until the signal returned before speaking. 'I don't think it'll get to you,' he said, frowning at the icon at the top of the phone display. 'We've got a very weak signal here. Any information on that roadblock, Mel?'

'Yeah,' came the reply. 'One police car was requested by Farid Galal to meet him on the outskirts of Laâyoune – the roadblock location according to the GPS.'

'But there are three cars there,' said Anna.

'Fake,' said Dan. 'Mel, keep a listen out – chances are, the officers who attended the call were shot at the scene and Galal's men are using other vehicles to man the roadblock. The call-out was simply to make it believable.'

He checked their progress away from the roadblock in his mirrors.

So far, so good.

'Dan, we've got a bigger problem,' said Mel, her tone urgent. 'We've just received word that all flights out of Laâyoune have been grounded.'

'Grounded?' Dan frowned and looked at Anna, who wore a similarly confused expression. 'Why?'

'Publicly, they're saying there's a security threat at the terminal,' said Mel. 'But the records I'm looking at state that this has been put in place at the request of the police.'

Dan ground his teeth. 'Is there a name for the police contact on file?'

'Yes,' said Mel. 'Farid Galal.'

Dan punched the wheel.

THIRTEEN

Galal tapped his radio against his chin and scowled at the vehicle at the front of the short queue.

One of his men held a flashlight, shining it in the faces of the driver and his passengers before straightening and waving the car on.

'Amir!' Galal called out. 'Enough. Let the rest of them pass.'

Amir held up his hand in response, then yelled at the other men to start moving their cars out of the way so the remaining traffic could pass.

The highway was soon deserted, save for Amir's men, and Galal wandered over to them.

'Have your men walk the highway,' he said, waving his hand in the direction of Bou Craa. 'No more than a mile. They must have left the road when they saw the roadblock.'

Amir's eyes narrowed as he stared into the distance. 'They won't get far,' he said. 'What do you think they're doing?'

'If I was them, I'd be trying to get to the airport by way of a back road,' said Galal, 'which is why there is currently a rumour at airport security about a potential terrorism threat.'

Amir smiled. 'Then they will not be able to leave the country.' He clenched his fist. 'And we will hunt them down.'

Galal's brow creased as his eyes swept the desert either side of the highway. His hands shook as he buttoned his jacket, and he forced himself to relax. It would do no good to let Amir see how scared he was. If he failed in his mission and the woman escaped, his punishment would be swift. And permanent.

'They could be anywhere out there,' he murmured.

'It will be light in a few hours,' said Amir. 'There is only a light wind tonight. If we find their tracks, we will be able to follow them.'

'How many of your men are in the area?'

'These six, plus I have two other groups of six in

the western and northern suburbs of Laâyoune,' said Amir.

'Contact them,' said Galal. 'Give them the details of Mr Taylor's vehicle. Tell them to patrol their areas.'

'And if they find him and the woman?'

'Tell them to kill them,' said Galal. 'I see no point in delaying the inevitable. We have her colleague's computer. We don't need anything from Miss Collins.'

'Understood.'

Galal watched Amir walk back to his men and issue their orders, the team immediately splitting up into two groups of three before taking a side of the road each and beginning their search.

Galal put the radio back in his car and stood with his arms folded across the roof of the vehicle as he watched the progress of Amir's men, their forms slowly fading into the blackness as they moved further away.

He cursed under his breath.

He had tried to prevent the stranger from leaving the mine camp without an escort, but the army captain had ruined his plans, asking procedural questions that any of the other policemen at the scene could have answered.

Something about the way in which the man had

hurried away from the site had piqued Galal's interest and as soon as he could, he had hurried back to the woman's bungalow to find the ventilation grille on the floor of the bathroom.

His masters would be displeased about his tactics since, but he was desperate – he simply couldn't allow the woman to leave the country with the information she held. It would destroy everything.

Two things were certain.

First, if he found Mr Taylor before Amir's men, he would have no hesitation in killing the Englishman himself.

Second, there was no way in hell Mr Taylor worked in insurance.

FOURTEEN

'We're going to have to overland it,' said Dan. 'There's no way we're going to be able to get to the airport. If this business with the mercenary force is as big as we think it is, then they're going to have lookouts for us on all routes leading to the international terminal. We'll never make it.'

'What about border patrols?' asked Mel.

'If Galal is linked to this Russian-backed mercenary force, then he's not going to go out of his way to bring in the real Moroccan army.' Dan glanced across at the young woman next to him. 'I have a feeling the only reason Anna survived the attack at the mine camp was because the army got there soon after Galal and his men.' He paused, reached out, and wrapped his fingers around

Anna's, knowing the words would frighten her. 'He used his own men to create the roadblocks and alert airport security because he can rely on his contacts within the police force.'

'You'll still have to out-run those mercenaries to get to the border,' said David.

'We've got a head start,' said Dan. 'Galal would've waited until he was sure why he didn't catch us at the roadblock. Then they'll have to follow our tracks. If I can find a way into the city that isn't on one of the main routes, then we can get some supplies and head out early morning. We'll sleep in the car tonight.'

'If you can get yourself to the border, I'll have someone meet you there,' said David. 'With the political situation in Western Sahara, we can't directly get involved. We'll have to wait until you reach Morocco.'

'What about the information on my laptop?' said Anna. 'I need to get that to my people.'

'And us,' said Mel. 'What do you need?'

'Access to a Wi-Fi connection or another satellite link if you have one,' said Anna. 'The satellite link would be better. It needs to be better than the signal we've got with this phone, though. The Internet connection in Western Sahara is appalling. That's why we couldn't alert our office to everything we'd found – it would've taken too long to upload.'

Dan heard her voice break and squeezed her shoulder.

Anna sniffed. 'It's why we decided it was better to leave the country immediately.'

'We're not going to be able to get a satellite connection for you there,' said David. 'Same issue. We can ensure that when you're met at the border that you have access to the Internet though. Dan? Is there anything else you need?'

'Negative,' said Dan. 'It's risky, but I'll have to use Mel's credit card to get some cash out in the city. We'll buy what we need to keep us going for a few days, just in case. I'll call you again when we're near the border. I don't want to waste the phone battery.'

'Understood,' said David. 'In that case, call us every twenty-four hours with your update, and again when you reach the border, unless it's urgent. We'll have someone on standby to meet you.'

'Copy that.'

'Best of luck, Dan.'

Dan ended the call and glanced across at Anna before his eyes returned to the horizon. The lights from the outer city limits loomed closer.

'I'll find somewhere to hide the car for the rest

of the night,' he said. 'Early tomorrow morning, we'll refuel and stock up on water, then make a run for the border, okay?'

Anna nodded. 'Do you think this will make it?' She patted the faux leather upholstery of the SUV.

Dan's lips thinned. 'Hope so,' he said. 'I don't fancy the alternative, do you?'

She shook her head.

'Okay,' said Dan, accelerating as the terrain levelled out and a cracked asphalt surface met the wheels, 'let's find somewhere to get our heads down for a few hours.'

'I don't think I'll be able to sleep.'

'You'll be surprised,' said Dan. 'And trust me, if you get the chance to sleep, take it.'

FIFTEEN

A distant radio hissed once before the tones of a *Gnaoua* song carried across the airwaves, a forlorn lament that stirred on the breeze, chasing after the sound of traffic that dispersed with the last notes of the local music.

Outside the moth-eaten apartment block, a group of men disappeared into the shadow of the building, leaving one of them on guard while the rest retired to a room at the back, bare except for the prayer mats that had been laid down in readiness.

A guard paced the area outside the front door, his eyesight keen, his footsteps carrying upwards to an open window on the third and highest level.

Gregori Abramov tuned out the background noise, bit into an apple, and sent a spray of juice over the computer keyboard under his fingers. He lifted his gaze to glare at the skinny twelve-year old kid that watched him wide-eyed from the doorway.

He could almost hear the boy salivating at the thought of tasting the fresh fruit, which was a luxury in the sprawling urban mass of Laâyoune – especially if you weren't a Moroccan ex-pat worker.

His thoughts turned to his own daughter, only a year older than the boy, her privileged lifestyle a stark contrast to that of the scrawny kid who watched him intently.

Abramov stopped chewing, the apple catching in his throat.

He'd received the first of the threats several months ago. In the lead-up to the theft of the money, the threats had increased.

Strangers were spotted in their exclusive neighbourhood in Moscow; his chauffeur had reported being followed as he'd driven Abramov's daughter to and from school, and his ex-wife had complained of phone calls late at night, only for her to answer and be met with silence at the end of the line.

Abramov wiped his chin, lowered his gaze, and finished the apple, tossing the core onto the table.

The boy's shoulders slumped before he eased away from the doorframe, and the Russian heard him pad away back down the passageway and out into the tiny communal courtyard.

He grunted in amusement and turned his attention back to the laptop. As he wiggled the mouse to activate the screen once more, the back of his hand brushed against the gun he kept near him at all times, the suppressor giving the weapon an elongated silhouette.

'It's okay? Everything is there?'

His head jerked up at the interruption, and he frowned.

Galal moved away from the window, his handprints left behind in the layer of dust that covered the sill where he'd been leaning, waiting for Abramov to hack into van Wyk's computer.

The Russian ignored the question. 'When will the security alert be lifted at the airport?'

The policeman jerked his arm from his shirt sleeve and checked his watch. 'Another hour.' He held up both hands, revealing dark sweat patches under his arms. 'That's all I can do, Gregori, without causing suspicion. I've got look-outs posted on all roads leading to the airport. They'll stay in position until we have the American woman.'

'Any fallout from the road block?'

Galal shook his head. 'The rumour about the insurance man is that he is a wanted terrorist in

Europe,' he said. 'He will be blamed for the cold-blooded killing of my men. The others will be well compensated.'

'Good. Where is Amjad Bassam?'

Galal shrugged. 'Still at the mine camp,' he said. 'They're treating it as a militant attack.' He chuckled. 'Don't worry, Gregori, no-one will know about your involvement.'

Abramov glared at the policeman. The man was presumptuous, and that made him dangerous. It meant he'd assume he was safe, and that Abramov in turn was untouchable.

Abramov assumed nothing. He planned, double-checked, and included for contingencies.

It ensured a thriving business, and in his line of work, reputation was everything.

He couldn't afford mistakes.

Abramov exhaled. However, it was much easier to work in a corrupted country, where bribes were recognised as an efficient way to do business, and the people you hired had no compunction about killing to get the job done.

That said, he would have preferred that Galal had managed to kill the forensic accountant and her supposed colleague.

He hated loose ends.

He pulled his handkerchief from his shirt

pocket, wiped his brow, and then punched another string of code into the laptop. Surely this time it would work.

His eyes flickered over the screen as a sequence ran its course, the algorithms seeking a way into the machine, probing for a clue to the information Abramov so desperately sought.

The digits and letters jumped down a line and then stopped, the cursor flashing expectantly.

He leaned back and swore.

Galal moved closer. 'What's the matter? What's wrong?'

Abramov didn't miss the note of panic in the other man's voice. His Russian temper preceded his reputation, and he'd quickly established a reign of fear amongst those he employed.

He picked up the laptop, stood, and then launched the useless computer at the opposite wall.

The plastic outer casing splintered on impact, carving out a sizeable dent from the decades-old plasterwork and sending shards of stonework scattering over the floor.

The policeman moved back towards the window, his hands seeking out the sill, and tried to put more distance between himself and the Russian.

Abramov forced his breathing under control

and rubbed his eyes before he turned and leaned his hands on the desk. 'Tell me again how they escaped, Galal.'

His right hand moved from the desk to the gun, and he caressed his fingers over the grip. 'What were there? Eight of you? Two of them?'

Galal's Adam's apple bobbed in his throat, and he took a step back. 'We believe the insurance man saw the road block and chose to escape across country.'

'He's not an 'insurance' man,' yelled Abramov.

'Please,' said Galal, holding his hands up, 'tell me what I can do to help.'

The Russian swung his arm around and shot the Moroccan in the chest. 'You can die,' he said.

He watched dispassionately as the policeman's body slumped to the floor, the man's hand travelling to the gaping wound between his ribs.

Galal's breath escaped his lips in a mottled gasp, blood flecking his chin as he stared at Abramov. His mouth worked, but no words came.

Abramov sighed, and aimed the gun at the policeman's head. 'Christ, you can't even die properly,' he muttered, and pulled the trigger.

He tucked the gun into his belt at the sound of running feet and turned as one of Galal's men appeared at the doorway, his eyes wide as he stared at the body of his boss.

Abramov pointed at him. 'Now you're in charge,' he snarled. 'Clean this mess up, and tell your men their orders have changed. Don't kill the woman when you find her. I need her alive.'

SIXTEEN

Dan exhaled and leaned against the wall of the building that led into the alleyway in which he'd parked the SUV only six hours ago.

Anna remained in the car, rubbing sleep from her eyes as he'd told her to stay put while he checked their surroundings. He'd heard the *clunk* of the internal locking mechanism as he'd strode towards the quiet street and, not for the first time, had silently thanked the general for ensuring his daughter had basic security training.

Not that he'd relax. Not until she was safely out of the country and on that plane home.

His brow creased as he monitored the street.

A café owner swept the pavement outside his business, a low whistle carrying on the air, while to

Dan's left, other shopkeepers began pulling their display counters from doors, ready to begin the day's trade.

While Anna had dozed fitfully, Dan had made a mental list of what they would need to complete their overland trip.

His plan was to buy their supplies from several businesses in the suburbs of Laâyoune – large purchases from any one store would mean their presence would be noted, and quite possibly passed onto Galal and his contacts.

While he observed the street growing busier as the trading hour drew near, Dan tried to recall everything he'd learnt about desert survival while in the British Army.

Water was an obvious essential. Food, less so – digesting food used up valuable moisture from a person's body, so he figured they could reduce their food intake with little discomfort. He planned to buy energy bars if he could: lightweight snacks as a back-up.

He'd found an ATM soon after entering the city and extracted as much cash as he could before driving for another hour to a suburb on the opposite side of the sprawling metropolis to park the vehicle overnight.

When Anna had queried the manoeuvre, he'd

explained that if Galal was monitoring their movements, then a large cash withdrawal from a bank would immediately draw his attention – and Dan wanted to be a long way from that location before they could be found.

Dan's head jerked to the left at a shout from further along the street, and then his shoulders relaxed as he saw the café owner hold up his hand to a neighbouring business owner. Loud banter ensued before the man waved and turned back to his shop and flipped the sign on the door to "Open."

Dan glanced over his shoulder.

Anna's eyes were wide as she watched him through the windscreen.

He smiled and gave her a thumbs-up, then turned and began to walk towards the café.

He'd already decided against using his broken Arabic to buy their supplies; the locals used a different form of the dialect, with some of the older generation maintaining Spanish as a second language – a trait from past colonial days. Dan figured it was simpler to stick to English and point to what he needed. He realised it would single him out further should Galal's contacts sweep the area in search of himself and Anna, but it was a quicker process, and one that meant they'd be on their way out of the city sooner.

He entered the café, nodded to the owner, and was relieved to see a glass-fronted refrigerator near the counter. He pulled out eight of the two-litre sized water bottles, put them on the counter and raised his eyebrow at the owner.

'How much are these?'

The owner frowned, shook his head, and then reached out for a scrap of paper and a pen next to the cash register. He scribbled on it, turned the page round to face Dan, and stabbed his finger at the amount he'd written down.

Dan chuckled, shook his head, and held out his hand for the pen.

The café owner scowled but acquiesced.

Dan wrote down a lower figure and pointed at it.

The café owner's bottom lip jutted out, but then he shrugged and nodded.

Dan grinned and handed over the cash. He pointed at an empty box that stood on the floor next to the owner's feet. 'Can I have that, please?'

The owner bent down and picked up the box, shoved it across the counter at Dan, then stood with his arms across his chest.

Dan sighed. *Small victories*, he reminded himself. 'Thanks,' he said.

He loaded the bottles, then took the box and

exited the café, checking the street as the door swung shut behind him.

The area was clear, no sign of anyone monitoring his movements, and the only pedestrians within his line of vision were the business owners he'd spotted before entering the café and a handful of early morning customers like himself.

He walked back to the SUV at a brisk pace, not too fast – just a Westerner returning to his accommodation with the day's supply of water.

Anna leaned forward across the dashboard as he rounded the corner and entered the alleyway. Before he reached the vehicle, she'd unlocked the doors once more, and he pushed the box of water bottles onto the back seat.

Climbing behind the wheel, he checked the mirrors and started the engine.

'Anyone show up while I was gone?'

'No,' said Anna.

She sounded out of breath, and her face was pale once more.

'Hang in there,' he said.

'I wasn't sure you'd come back.' She shook her head. 'Stupid, I know.'

'It's okay to be scared,' said Dan. 'It'll keep you

alert. But don't let your fear turn to panic.' He smiled. 'And by the way, I'd never leave you. You're stuck with me.'

Anna managed a small smile. 'Good.'

'Right. Next stop.'

Dan braked as the vehicle exited the alleyway, then turned into the street and increased his speed. He tilted his wrist towards him, checking the time. He wanted to be out of the city before the larger businesses such as banks and the like opened their doors for the morning's trade.

No doubt Galal would be seeking assistance from the banks to see if a large sum of money had been removed from an ATM that day, and Dan had no intention of being anywhere in the city when he found the information he sought. Despite making his purchases several miles away from the cash machine, Dan preferred to err on the side of caution.

And therefore caution dictated he be the hell out of Laâyoune before nine o'clock.

He drummed his fingers on the steering wheel as he criss-crossed the streets, looking for a store that would sell the items he needed. He'd hoped to avoid the city centre, preferring to skirt around the smaller pockets of shops around the outer perimeter, but after half an hour of searching, he knew it was pointless.

'We need a camping store,' he said to Anna. 'I want to buy some emergency supplies – water purification tablets, extra layers of clothing for us. Keep your eyes peeled.'

'Okay.'

Anna sat up straighter in her seat, her eyes flickering over the shops they passed and down side streets as the road became more congested with traffic.

Dan ignored the sweat that began to tickle the back of his neck. The closer they got to the city centre, the more likely it was their vehicle would be spotted and reported.

A store on his side of the road caught his eye, and he braked suddenly, swinging the SUV next to the kerb.

Anna looked around, her eyes wide. 'What is it? Is it them?'

'Relax,' said Dan, and pointed through the windscreen. 'I need to go to that shop over there. Lock the doors again.'

'Oh. Okay.'

'Won't be long.'

He slammed the car door and strode across the

pavement towards the shop, its window display uniformly tidy and nondescript.

Pushing open the door, he was immediately struck by the silence in the space, which offered an almost cocoon-like sanctuary from the noise and heat outside.

An elderly man shuffled out from a back room at the sound of a bell above the door, his hands clasped in front of him.

Dan pointed towards the mannequins in the window display and then pointed at himself before indicating a shorter person.

The man's brow furrowed, and then he held up a finger and smiled. He nodded and beckoned Dan towards the counter, where he dragged out two pre-packaged black robes, one an extra-large size from what Dan could make of the labels, and one a petite size.

Dan nodded and indicated he'd take both. A similar transaction to that for more water bottles ensued, and five minutes later Dan hammered on the window of the SUV.

Anna jumped in her seat before reaching out and releasing the locks. She frowned when Dan handed her the packages.

'Black? I would've thought white would have been a better colour in this heat.'

Dan started the engine and pulled away from the kerb before turning the vehicle down the first side street he could, happier to be away from the main road and prying eyes.

'White reflects heat,' he explained. 'Black absorbs it – and your body's own heat, so it's a cooler option. Especially away from the city and any shade. If we do have to get out of the vehicle for any reason, covering yourself from head to toe in black material is a much better option.'

Anna gazed out of the window. 'I forgot you were in Iraq.'

'It was a long time ago.'

'But you haven't forgotten.'

'No. I learned a lot from the locals,' Dan said. 'We all did.'

Ten minutes later, he finally found the camping store he'd been seeking and bought the last of the supplies.

As he started the engine for the last time, he peered across the seats at Anna. 'Last chance to say no.'

He saw her swallow, and she appeared to gauge her response before answering.

'Given the alternative, I'd rather take my chances,' she said at last. 'If we don't get out of this country and tell the UK government what's going on down here, no-one else will.' Her face fell. 'Not now that Benji is dead.'

Dan slipped his sunglasses over his eyes. 'Ready?'

Anna nodded. 'Let's get out of here.'

'Copy that.'

SEVENTEEN

Dan pointed the SUV in the direction of one of the north-eastern suburbs of Laâyoune and weaved the vehicle through the side streets, avoiding main roads wherever he could. The inhabitants of the city were arriving at work, and he was fifteen minutes over his self-imposed deadline.

Within minutes, phones would start ringing in busy offices, questions would be asked, bribes would be taken, and he and Anna would become easy targets if they remained in the area for much longer.

He found a road leading directly north, the residential area becoming more and more sparse before the city finally spat them out of its clutches.

They'd been driving on dust and dirt for the

past mile, and once the city had become a speck in his rear view mirrors, Dan finally relaxed his hands on the steering wheel and let the vehicle suspension take the strain of the uneven surface.

Anna picked up on his mood and sighed. 'I didn't think we'd ever get away,' she said.

'It's still early,' said Dan, 'so with any luck it'll take them a few hours to pick up our trail. I want to put as much distance between them and us while we still can. It'll be too dangerous to drive overland at night, so we'll keep going as long as possible and then try to find somewhere we can hide the vehicle.'

'I can drive for a bit if you want.'

Dan nodded. Anna's father had a large ranch in the Arizona desert, and from an early age Anna had learned how to handle the four-wheel drive vehicles the farmhands used to manage the property.

'Be my guest. Two hours each?'

'Sure.'

Dan shuffled in his seat, got his long legs comfortable in the foot well, and thanked David's foresight in hiring a vehicle with an automatic transmission. Driving a manual over the uneven terrain would have been exhausting.

'How did you end up working in Rotterdam?' he asked. 'Last time I saw you, you still had a year to go at university.'

Anna smiled. 'Yeah, and by the end of it I decided if I was going to be an accountant, I wanted some excitement with it.' She bounced her fist off the window. 'I didn't expect this, though,' she added as she stared out at the bleak landscape passing them.

Dan could see that it'd take a long time for her to recover from what she'd been through the previous day, and he pressed on, hoping it would help her to talk about it. From personal experience, he knew it would do her no good to bottle up her feelings, and Anna was well aware of the demons he'd battled in the past.

'So,' he said. 'How did you end up in Western Sahara? I mean, I know you got a call from the mine development company's insurers, but surely you could've carried out your investigation from your office.'

'Only up to a point.' Anna brought her knees up to her chin and wrapped her arms around them, kicked her shoes off, and curled her toes. 'Like I said when we spoke to David and Mel, the Internet access here in Western Sahara is atrocious. We're only an hour ahead of them in The Netherlands, but the insurer was becoming more and more frustrated at the length of time it was taking to conduct the investigation – they needed fast results;

their client was waiting to be reimbursed, and at the same time its head office in Houston was being investigated by the FBI to make sure nothing untoward happened at that end.'

'Had it?'

'No. They were clean. It was definitely a remote attack, but somehow linked to the new mine here.'

'What happened next?'

'My boss caved in – agreed with the client to send Benji and me down here to see if we could speed up the investigation by auditing the in-house systems.' She sniffed. 'Benji was a computer whizz-kid. They'd employed him even before he'd left university – he worked part-time for them until he graduated. If anyone could find out where that money went, it was him.'

'What was your role?'

'To collate the information in such a way that it could be audited and verified,' she said. 'It falls to me to decide whether the insurance client reimburses the mine development company, or whether we decide that they were negligible in their actions and therefore responsible for the missing money.'

'How *did* it go missing?'

'Some malware virus had been placed on the

system – pretty easy to do with a link in an email to a website that then bounces back an error message.'

'Yeah, seen that before.'

'Right. So, once that malware had been installed, all the hackers had to do was intercept all the emails, review them, and wait until one of the suppliers' accounts departments contacted the mine development company with its bank details for payment. The hackers then intercepted it, changed the bank details to their own, and waited for the money to arrive.'

'Shit. That easy?'

'Yeah. Most hackers do a test run first though, to see if it'll work and if they'll get away with it. This particular theft happened with the whole of the second milestone payment, so we went back and checked the first one.'

'And?'

'It was fifty dollars short when the money arrived in the supplier's bank account.'

'And no-one said anything?'

Anna shrugged. 'Someone somewhere made a business decision. The mining industry's been struggling for the past six years – suppliers are desperate for work. They're not going to argue over a missing fifty dollars. It'll simply get added to the bad debtors figure in the annual accounts.'

Dan blinked. 'That's incredible. Why isn't every hacker in the world doing this?'

Anna smiled. 'Who's to say they're not? Companies rarely report it to the media. Too embarrassing.'

'So, you arrived here thinking you were simply going to identify the hackers – and then, what? Report them to Interpol or something?'

'Exactly. We build a criminal case and then pass it onto the authorities, including the FBI and Interpol. The insurance company – our client – then has to hope that a prosecution occurs.'

'When did you realise you were in trouble? What was it that tipped you off?'

'We found out that other projects in the region were missing money – like I said, no-one was talking openly about it, but Benji and I made some discreet enquiries and found out that a couple of our competitors were in the country, doing exactly the same thing as us.'

'And that led you to the conclusion that the funds had been stolen to fund a local uprising.'

Anna nodded. 'Usually, when money is stolen like this, it's sent as far away as possible from the scene of the original theft. All these thefts were different – the money was coming back, or being sent to individuals with interests in Western

Sahara. The organisation I work for has some ex-military contacts, so I managed to make some phone calls two days ago to see if they had heard anything via their network of colleagues. I got a message yesterday morning that confirmed my suspicions – someone is actively contacting known mercenaries, particularly those from Russia and Eastern Europe, and offering large sums of money to discreetly make their way into Western Sahara.'

Dan cricked his neck before he pushed his sunglasses up onto his head and rubbed at his eyes.

'Do you want me to drive for a while?'

Dan checked his mirrors. There were no vehicles following them.

'Yeah, that'd be good.'

He slowed and brought the SUV to a gentle stop, and they switched sides.

Dan stretched before he climbed into the passenger seat.

After a few seconds of each of them adjusting their seats to account for their difference in height, Anna released the handbrake and set off.

'You haven't told me what you've been up to,' she said, as she tilted the rear view mirror to better suit her line of sight. 'Still trying to save the world?'

Dan glanced across and narrowed his eyes at the dimples that had appeared in Anna's cheeks.

'I'll have you know I was doing very important work for the British government,' he said in mock indignation.

She laughed, and Dan smiled.

'You said "was,"' she said.

'Yeah.' Dan pulled his sunglasses over his eyes. 'The last job didn't go too well.'

Anna's eyes flickered across to him before she spoke.

'Well, that's not exactly encouraging news.'

EIGHTEEN

Jamil Iqbal lowered the binoculars from his eyes and squinted into the distance.

From his position, he could easily spot the plume of sand and dust the Englishman's hired vehicle spat into the air.

He clambered down from the hood of his battered pick-up truck, walked round to the driver's door, and passed the binoculars through the open window.

'It's them,' he said.

'You're sure?'

Jamil grinned, revealing a row of rotten teeth. 'No-one else would be stupid enough to drive through here,' he said.

'True.'

The driver peered through the windscreen at the disappearing dust trail.

'What do you want to do?' asked Jamil. His fingers tapped impatiently on the door frame. 'Shall we follow?'

The driver thought for a moment. 'No. They're only going to be able to drive a few more miles before they'll have to stop.' He glanced at the cheap watch wrapped around his wrist, and then at the shadows forming under the scrubby bushes to the right of the stationary vehicle. 'It'll be dark in a few hours. If they try to keep driving when the sun goes down, it'll be suicide.'

'So they'll have to double back?'

'Eventually.' The driver placed the binoculars in a crevasse in the central console. 'Get in. Use the radio to call Salim. Let him know he's going to have visitors soon.'

Jamil hurried round to the passenger door and wrenched it open, hissing as the hot leather upholstery burned through his thin trousers, and picked up the UHF radio. He turned the dial until it reached a little-used frequency and spoke rapidly into the microphone, his glee at finding the man and woman barely disguised.

The driver started the engine, rolled up his

window, and turned the wheel, pointing the vehicle in an easterly direction.

The man and woman would be stopped eventually, and then they'd have to turn around and find a new route.

And he and his men would be waiting for them.

Abramov replaced the radio in its cradle and shivered from an involuntary chill that wasn't caused by the gradual drop in air temperature, but by the thought that the safety of his daughter was clouding his judgement.

For previous contracts, he'd never risked using local enforcements, especially any as ill-trained as those that Galal had recruited on his behalf.

Secretly, he harboured a suspicion that Salim's men were somehow related to Galal, and he'd simply allowed blood ties to dictate who was added to the payroll.

Normally, Abramov would select his men: hand-picked fighters who he'd bet his life on.

But the client had been very clear in his expectations.

Nothing was to be traced back to the mother country. The leader could not afford to be tainted by the success or failure of the mission – he could only be seen as a saviour as the occupied territory tore itself apart in a brutal civil war.

Abramov clenched his fists. There would be no civil war if he couldn't recruit skilled mercenaries from the local population.

Abramov had been limited to bringing only six of his men, despite a loud and frustrating meeting with two of the client's representatives.

After the meeting, they'd made it clear that would be the only concession and that Abramov was not in a position to negotiate further with them.

It was then that Abramov set a plan in motion to secure the safety of his daughter.

Now, his gaze met the eyes of every single member of his six-man team.

'Get ready to leave,' he said. 'The minute Salim confirms he has them, we travel to his base. In the meantime, monitor the radios in case the Englishman and the American woman manage to evade capture.'

NINETEEN

Dan peered over the top of his sunglasses, his gaze wandering between the view out his driver's side window, the front windscreen, and the rear view mirror.

Everywhere he looked, the yellow russet tones of the desert spread before him, cacti and gourd breaking up the desert in sporadic patches for as far as he could see.

Now and then, a collection of large coloured boulders appeared on the horizon, the vehicle passing through the shade they cast as he steered a safe passage across the rough terrain. His geologist mind turned to thoughts of ancient causeways, glacial shifts that had cast the boulders from mountains thousands of miles away.

He frowned and pushed his sunglasses back up his nose, peering past the slumbering form of Anna towards the west, where the sun was rapidly making a run for the horizon.

His eyes flickered over the scenery in front of him as he guided the SUV through a shallow gulley, carved out through time by water before the desert encroached, and then no doubt used as a goat track by passing herdsmen.

He pulled a bottle of water from the cup holder to his left and took a long drink. He calculated how much they'd used over the course of the day and estimated that it'd take another half day's driving to reach the border. They had plenty of fluids to keep them going, but they were already dehydrating in the exposed environment, notable since neither of them had stopped to go to the toilet in the past four hours.

He put the bottle back and checked his mirrors.

He wondered what Galal was planning. No doubt the man was only a small pawn in a bigger game, but he had local knowledge – and influence.

And Dan had no idea as to how large the group of mercenaries was.

He recalled a news article he'd read over the past few months about Western Sahara. The UN had renewed its resolution to keep a watching brief on the territory and choosing to ignore Morocco's occupation, to the frustration of the country's Polisario group who represented the local Sahrawi people.

At the heart of everything was the very real threat from a growing Al Qaeda presence in the northern reaches of the region and corruption within the local army.

Even if any attempt by a mercenary force to tip the geo-political balance failed, it would open up the country to further Al Qaeda influence.

An influence that the rest of the world could ill afford.

Dan reached out and switched the headlights onto a low beam as the light outside began to fade and the last of the sun's rays spread out across the sky.

His attention taken by the stunning scene, he turned back to the windscreen and shouted in surprise.

He stamped on the brake pedal, the back of the SUV sliding sideways at the sudden deceleration.

Anna jolted forward, straining against her seatbelt at the sudden stop, her head jerking forwards as she was jolted from her sleep.

As the dust settled around the now stationary

vehicle, Anna blinked, and then spun in her seat to face him.

'What happened?' she demanded, her hair in disarray.

'That,' said Dan, and pointed towards the front of the vehicle.

Anna's eyes followed his hand.

Only a couple of metres from the limit of the vehicle's headlights, a sign stood sentinel on a lone post, its message in stark red lettering in both Arabic and English.

Danger! Mine Field. Do Not Enter.

Dan felt the tremor begin in his legs and rested his palms on his knees in an effort to disguise his fear.

It had been several years, but the scars still peppered his chest and back, pale jagged stripes that cut swathes across his sun-tanned skin.

He swallowed in an attempt to counteract the dryness of his mouth and tried to ignore the prickle of goose bumps on his forearms.

'What do we do?' said Anna.

Dan ran his hand across his mouth.

There was no way in hell he was going to attempt to cross the minefield – it would be suicide.

Somehow, he had to find another way to cross the border into Morocco.

He checked his watch.

It was over eight hours since they'd left the city, and it would be dark soon.

He shoved the SUV's transmission into reverse and yanked the steering wheel to a hard right.

'We'll keep as far away from this boundary as we can,' he said. 'The sun's going to go down within the hour. It'll be too dangerous to drive by then – we could wander into the minefield by accident.'

Anna turned in her seat to face him. 'They'll be following us by now, won't they?'

Dan nodded. 'I expect so. It's still too dangerous to carry on, though.' He hit the brakes. 'Let's see if anyone's within sight.'

He grabbed the binoculars and opened his door, stepping out onto the running board and turning towards the way they had travelled.

The flat terrain spread out behind them, affording Dan an uninterrupted view.

Nothing moved.

He lowered the binoculars, his mind racing, and then turned and raised them once more, in the direction the vehicle pointed.

He adjusted the focus.

'That might do,' he murmured.

'What?'

He passed the binoculars to Anna and pointed

to his one o'clock position. 'That looks like a low rock ledge,' he said. 'We might be able to get the vehicle under it. Try to get our heads down for a few hours.'

Dan pulled the black material around his shoulders and stared out over the sandy expanse towards the mine field.

A shiver wracked his body as old memories surfaced, of improvised explosive devices planted within footsteps of main pedestrian thoroughfares, designed to maim and kill with as much destruction as possible.

He clenched his fist, bunching the material between his fingers as his jaw tightened, the old demons threatening to surface. He tried to concentrate instead on taking his bearings from the stars, thankful that he'd kept up his navigation skills during the time he'd spent on the boat rather than constantly relying on GPS.

'Dan?'

He jumped, his right hand falling to the Glock at his hip, before he shook his head and forced himself to focus.

Anna stood over him, concern etched across her

features in the pale moonlight.

'The nightmares are back, aren't they?'

Dan exhaled. 'I'm okay.'

Anna lowered herself until she was sitting beside him. 'No. You're not.'

'It's just the minefield. It brought back memories.'

'I thought it had,' she said. She reached out and squeezed his shoulder. 'You haven't been the same since you saw the sign.'

She moved closer, until she could wrap her arm around him, and rested her head on his shoulder.

Dan shifted and rubbed his cheek on her hair. 'I didn't think you'd remember about the nightmares.'

She sniffed. 'I was scared at first,' she said, 'when you came to stay with us. You towered over me. You were – are – so imposing. But, at night...' She lifted her head so her eyes met his. 'You cried out, like you were still in so much pain.'

'Shh,' said Dan. He traced his fingers over her hair until she lowered her gaze and rested against his shoulder once more.

He knew she meant well, but now wasn't the time to start psychoanalysing his memories.

He had to stay focused, protect Anna, and get them both through whatever faced them the following day.

'I'm okay,' he said. 'We can do this.'

TWENTY

Dan ran his hand over the dusty tyre tread, then straightened and moved to the next wheel, his eyes assessing the wear and tear the vehicle had suffered the previous day.

He was surprised how well the SUV was handling the terrain and resolved to maintain their steady progress when they set off once more.

They'd woken at dawn from fitful sleep, the cold morning air seeping through the extra layers he'd purchased. They each devoured a cereal bar while they leaned against the vehicle, sipping from water bottles, and watched the sun begin to rise.

He glanced over his shoulder to a group of shrubs several metres from where he stood, to see Anna emerge, her hair re-tied into a ponytail.

'Everything okay?' he said as she drew near.

'Yes, thanks.' She managed a smile. 'Not quite like camping in Arizona, though.' She joined him as he finished checking the vehicle and shielded her eyes from the sunlight as she peered back towards the direction of the minefield. 'What's the plan?'

Dan held up his smartphone. 'Time to check in.'

Anna stayed by his side as he hit the speed dial. David answered at the second ringtone.

'Dan?'

'Morning.'

'Where are you?'

'Near a minefield about a hundred miles east of Laâyoune,' said Dan. 'I'm aiming to find a road that will head north out of the country. Can you have someone meet us over the border?'

'Negative, Dan.' Mel's voice came on the line. 'You'll need to think of something else. There's a heavy police presence on the highways at the moment. Seems Galal hasn't given up yet.'

'I thought that might happen. Damn it.' Dan kicked a stone at his feet, sending it hurtling over the ground. 'Right, there have to be manned border posts up and down this route near the berm – we just have to find one we can access without going near the mines. Galal might have the police going round in circles, but maybe we stand a better chance with the army.'

'Do you think that's possible?' said David.

'I don't know. I would imagine most of the border posts are manned from the Moroccan side, but there might be a way through.'

'Dan? That's going to be impossible,' said Mel. 'When the Moroccans built the berm, they laid a minefield the whole length of it. The signs you saw are only the start. And, even if you did manage to get through, there are still barbed wire and electric fences – you'd never get near one of the command posts.'

Dan exhaled. 'Okay, Plan B. We keep travelling east anyway, and cross into Algeria.'

'Risky,' said David, 'but if you can get to Tindouf, there's a UN compound there – sort of a watching brief next to the refugee camp. Reach that, and we can arrange transportation back over the border into Morocco. Galal's influence won't reach that far. I can't see a way for you to track back to the UN base at Samara without being seen by the police.'

Dan looked away from Anna, and his eyes travelled back the way they'd driven. So far, there had been no sign of Galal or anyone else in pursuit.

All they had done was maintain a presence on the main highways.

It worried him, especially after the coordinated attack on the mining camp. It didn't seem in their enemies' nature to let them escape, not after going to such lengths to arrange first the roadblock, then the security alert at the country's biggest airport.

'How far is it to Tindouf?' asked Anna.

'About four hundred miles,' said David.

'Oh.' She took a step back and surveyed the vehicle. 'Will it make it?'

'We'll have to take it easy,' said Dan. 'So far, there are no oil or water leaks.'

'But we'll need fuel.'

'Exactly.' He held up his smartphone, the signal wavering despite Mel's satellite link, the battery icon showing two-thirds of the power remaining. He thumbed through the icons on the screen until he found the map one and held it out so Anna could see. 'There's a small town south of our current position. It's not on a main road, so we'll have to take our chances. We'll top up the fuel there, buy extra in jerry cans to strap to the roof, and then pick up our route again.'

Anna rested her hands on her hips as she cast her eyes over the desert landscape. 'It'll take us, what, another day and a half, you think?'

'Based on our progress yesterday, yes. Say two, given that we have to detour first to get fuel.'

'Okay.' She turned back to him and nodded. 'Let's do it.'

'You hear that, David?' said Dan.

'Affirmative,' came the reply. 'Again, suggest you take your bearings from your current position, then switch off your phone to conserve power. Call us in twenty-four hours with your position. Sooner if you need us. We'll be standing by.'

'Copy that.'

Dan ended the call and turned to Anna. 'Right,' he said. 'Let's go.'

TWENTY-ONE

'So, why haven't they started their attacks?' asked Dan as the SUV bounced across the desert terrain.

He shifted down a gear and accelerated up a small incline. 'If they've got their men in place, surely they'd want to start the uprising now, then get the hell out of here before anyone works out what's going on?'

Anna pursed her lips. 'It's a cash flow problem.'

'What do you mean?'

'Benji had an encryption code he'd developed. Remember I told you he was recruited as a teenager?'

'Yeah.'

'He was a natural with computers.' Anna sniffed before clearing her throat. 'Anyway, once we found out what bank account the stolen money was going into and being distributed out of, Benji locked it down.'

'He did what? Is that even possible?'

'Everything's connected,' she said. 'Once you're behind the wire, you can do anything.' Anna closed her eyes. 'It was the first thing he did that morning. He fully intended to release the money if we'd made a mistake in our investigation – it could easily be blamed on a bank error. In the meantime, all the money that was going to pay for any uprising or for weapons has been frozen.'

Dan emitted a low whistle. 'No wonder they're pissed off with you.' He squinted at the horizon. 'We might still have time to stop it, then.'

Anna turned to him and nodded. 'If they don't find us first, yes.'

Dan exhaled. Anna's discovery of the cyber theft and then her colleague's attempt to freeze the assets may have slowed down the hackers; it certainly wouldn't stop them. Not with the tantalising incentive of tilting the balance in the region to gain a stronghold over a lucrative export market.

He blinked as something shone in his eyes from the horizon, and breathed a sigh of relief.

'This must be it,' he said, pointing through the windscreen.

As they neared, the small township revealed itself to be nothing more than a motley collection of sandy-coloured buildings, each with a flat roof to collect what scant rainwater might pass through the region. Tiny windows pierced the walls, letting as little sunlight in as possible during the scorching hours of daylight.

Two large communications masts poked between the buildings, rising up into the sky for several metres, a strobe light affixed to the top of each to warn any low-flying aircraft of their presence.

Dan slowed the SUV to a crawl as they left the rocky terrain and drove onto the dusty track that led into the township.

He checked his watch. Mid-morning, and the single main street appeared deserted.

His gut twisted.

'What do they do here?' said Anna. 'There's no-one around.'

'I don't know,' said Dan. 'Keep your eyes open for somewhere we might be able to buy some fuel and water. We're not going to hang around.'

'Good.'

Dan kept the SUV at a steady pace as they

traversed an intersection, the main road criss-crossing an identical dusty street.

'When I was little, Dad took me to a mock-up of a Wild West town close to where we lived,' said Anna. 'This feels just like it. I'm half expecting to see four guys with shotguns appear in the street to run us out of town.'

'Yeah, I know what you mean,' said Dan, his eyes scanning the buildings. 'And I don't like it.'

He sat up straighter in his seat and increased his speed. 'Looks like we're in luck, though.'

He jerked his head towards a sign erected on a high pole further up the road, a familiar oil company logo faded from the harsh desert sunlight.

'It looks like it's closed.'

'It's open,' said Dan. 'Look.'

He pointed towards the low building that stood behind the fuel bowsers, a battered and torn awning strung above the entrance.

Next to the doorway, a man sat in a canvas chair, his hand shielding his eyes as he stared at the unfamiliar vehicle.

Dan reached for the keys and turned off the engine. His hand on the door release, he glanced at Anna.

'Lock the doors when I get out.'

He pulled his sunglasses from his face as he stepped from the vehicle. The sun was blinding, but from his experiences in the Army in the Middle East, he knew it could mean the difference between getting help or being ignored. An early instructor of his had told him that being able to look someone in the eyes rather than be confronted with the anonymity of sunglasses often broke through cultural barriers.

He hoped to hell it worked as well in Western Sahara as it had in other countries he'd been posted to.

He approached the man in the canvas chair, who flapped an old newspaper in front of his face while he fought a losing battle with the flies that gathered around him.

The man peered at him through hooded eyes that flitted between Dan and the vehicle.

Dan gestured to the fuel bowsers in the courtyard, then drew out some cash from his pocket and held it up.

The man grunted, tossed his newspaper to one side, and eased out of his chair.

He snatched the money from Dan's hand and beckoned him towards the fuel bowsers and the waiting car.

Dan followed, signalled to Anna to unlock the

doors, and reached in to pull the fuel cap release before joining the man at the pump.

The owner pointed at the two pumps and raised an eyebrow.

One had a black sticker next to the dial, the other a yellow one.

Dan pointed at the yellow one, and hoped he wasn't about to wreck the engine by having diesel pumped into the tank.

He left the man to top up the fuel, having agreed a price for an extra jerry can of fuel by waving more cash at the man and gesturing to the empty cans lined up next to the door of the office. Working his way round to the driver's side once more, he leaned in, pulled the catch to release the hood, and carried out a thorough check of the oil and water levels.

All good. No surprises.

Dan dropped the lid to find the man staring at him and took a step back.

'Okay?'

The man nodded.

'Great, thanks.'

Dan slipped behind the steering wheel, started the engine, and turned the vehicle back into the road.

'Let's get the hell out of Dodge,' he said.

TWENTY-TWO

Dan kicked at the tyre and cursed out loud in four different languages.

They'd travelled less than an hour before the vehicle's steering had turned sloppy, and he'd pulled over, suspecting a puncture.

It was only when he was fetching the jack and the spare wheel from the back of the SUV that he'd looked down and noticed that the other back tyre was flat too.

He'd dropped to the ground and run his hand over the rubber surface, and discovered the tiny nick from a knife deep within the tread.

Anna rounded the corner of the vehicle and shaded her eyes from the sun as she crouched down beside him.

'Puncture?'

Dan shook his head. 'Sabotage,' he said, and pointed out the identical cuts in each back tyre. He stood, threw the jack and spare tyre back into the vehicle, and slammed the door shut. 'Fuck it.'

'The man at the garage?'

'Yeah. Bastard.'

He ran his eyes over the landscape they'd travelled, and then spun on his heel and surveyed what lay ahead.

It didn't look promising.

In the heat of the day, a harmattan haze spread across the horizon, restricting visibility and hampering any attempt to gauge what lay ahead.

'I guess they don't have roadside assistance out here,' said Anna.

He snorted. 'No, I guess not.' He opened the back door to the vehicle and began pulling their belongings from the seat. 'Can you strip down your laptop computer? Take out the hard drive?'

'Why?'

'We can't stay here. The tyres have been slashed on purpose. So, we need to walk and put as much distance as we can between us and the vehicle before someone finds it.' He squinted into the distance, back towards the small settlement they'd left behind. 'Priority has to be water, so we carry all of it between us.' His gaze returned to Anna. 'So just take the parts of the laptop you need.'

'Okay.'

Anna reached into her backpack and extracted the computer, then turned it over and frowned.

'What's wrong?'

She held it up so Dan could see.

'I need a screwdriver.'

'No you don't. Give it here.'

Dan took the laptop from her, then raised it above his head and threw it to the ground at his feet.

The plastic casing splintered on impact, scattering components across the dirt.

Anna scrambled for the hard drive and tucked it into the pocket of her backpack before standing up and facing Dan. 'So much for the warranty.'

'I'll buy you a new one.'

'I'm counting on it.'

He grinned as she tried to look angry. 'I'll take you to the best computer store in Phoenix, promise.'

Anna put her hand on her hip. 'What is it you English say? *Bollocks*?'

Dan laughed. 'Come on. Let's hustle.' He pulled out all the water bottles from the back seat of the car and distributed them between his pack and

Anna's, taking the majority of the weight for himself. 'What else do you need to take?'

'It doesn't matter,' she said, testing the weight of her backpack and taking another water bottle from him. 'Most of what I need is up here.' She tapped the side of her head.

'What do you mean?'

She shrugged. 'I erred on the side of caution,' she said. 'I don't know – call it gut instinct if you like – but I had a feeling we were being watched the moment we set foot in the country. So, I didn't put everything in my report to head office yesterday. Only enough to give them the broader picture.' She held up the hard drive. 'It's all on here.' She grinned. 'And no-one can access the funds without the passwords Benji gave me, anyway.'

Dan swallowed and turned away, busying himself with the final preparations to leave the vehicle while his mind churned over what Anna had said.

And the fact that if their enemies realised she held the key to their demise, they'd stop at nothing to wring it from her.

His fists clenched, and he shook his head, trying to clear the thought.

He *had* to get her to safety.

'Here.' He passed one of the black robes to her,

then climbed out of the vehicle and draped his own robe over his head and shoulders.

Anna copied him, folding the end of the robe over her mouth and nose in an attempt to protect her face from the sun.

'Right, let's check in with David before we head off,' said Dan, and pulled out his mobile phone. He frowned when he saw the battery level but dialled the number anyway.

When David answered, Mel next to him on speakerphone, Dan relayed what had happened with the SUV, and his plan to start walking in the hope they would find a small settlement where they could pay a driver to take them the rest of the way to Tindouf.

'Dan? You don't stand a chance. She's never done this, and your experience is nearly a decade old.'

Dan jostled the phone in his hand as he passed another full water bottle to Anna. 'We'll be fine. Anna's grown up in the Arizona desert, and I've trained with the general there.' He exhaled as his eyes fell to the sabotaged tyres. 'We have to keep moving.'

Anna stuffed the last bottle into the side of her backpack, then hoisted the bag onto her shoulders and raised her hands. 'Ready?'

He pressed the phone closer to his ear. 'We don't have a choice. I'll update you on our progress when I can.'

'Wait.'

Dan held his breath, biting back a retort that might not be required. He heard Mel's voice in the background, her tone urgent, and then David returned to the phone.

'Mel's located a UN airstrip at Mahbes – it's closer than Tindouf. If you can get there, we can organise transportation to the border near there to collect you. It'll take some persuading back here, but I'll pull some strings. There are a few people around here who still owe me favours.'

'Thanks, David.' Dan checked his watch. 'Okay, we're out of here. I want to get as many miles as possible between us and them before nightfall.'

TWENTY-THREE

Three hours later, Dan and Anna trudged over a low ridge of rocks and boulders, their progress hampered by the unevenness of the ground under their feet.

Dan wrapped the robe around his nose and mouth tighter as the wind lifted it from his shoulders.

A dust devil danced in the sand at his feet, and his eyes scanned the horizon.

The thought of a sandstorm ripping across the desert filled him with dread. They simply wouldn't survive.

Anna had slowed, but Dan said nothing and matched his pace to hers.

Despite the robe covering his face, he could still

taste the gritty sand between his teeth. When they'd stopped to take a drink an hour before, he'd taken a small sip to start with before spitting it out in an attempt to clear his mouth. Ten minutes after setting off again, the sand was back.

They'd stopped talking half an hour ago and instead concentrated on putting one foot in front of the other, Dan's hand reaching out to steady Anna when she'd stumbled on a protruding rock.

She'd mumbled her thanks and then set off once more looking even more determined.

Dan admired her resolve. She wasn't a quitter, and she didn't complain.

Dan adjusted the backpack on his shoulders, the jangle of zips breaking the heavy silence that wrapped itself around them. Their footsteps sank into the dry earth, kicking up clouds around their ankles as they trudged forwards.

He licked his lips, already cracked from exposure to the harsh sunlight, and stopped.

'Water break,' he said.

Anna sighed and let her own backpack drop to the ground at her feet.

Dan reached down and picked out one of the full bottles from her pack to reduce the weight she carried.

'Here. Small sips. We share this one.'

She nodded and took the bottle from him.

He swallowed in unison as she sipped from the bottle, his tongue rasping against the roof of his dry mouth. Finally, Anna wiped the back of her mouth, then used her shirt to wipe the bottle top, and held it out to him.

Dan had to stop himself from ignoring his own advice. Every cell in his body demanded rehydration, and it was all he could do not to tip his head back and drain the lot.

Instead, he took sips, the warm water flushing some of the grit from his teeth and lips. Too soon, and his ration was gone.

'No food?' asked Anna, her eyes hopeful.

He shook his head. 'Not until the sun starts to go down,' he said. 'Eating causes us to use more water from our bodies to digest the food. We need to stay as hydrated as possible.'

He scrunched up the empty bottle and shoved it into his backpack next to two more, then hefted it on to his shoulders, grateful that Anna hadn't asked him why he didn't simply throw the bottles away.

There was no use in leaving a trail for their enemies to follow.

A motley collection of wind-torn shrubs stood to their left-hand side, and Anna sighed with relief.

'I need to pee,' she said.

'Go for it,' said Dan.

He wandered several metres past the bushes and kept his back turned as he surveyed the landscape beyond their position. He checked his watch, took his bearings, and contemplated where they might shelter overnight.

The terrain was bad enough to cross by vehicle, and he wasn't prepared to risk one of them spraining an ankle trying to gain a few more miles in the dark.

'Dan?'

He stopped at the note of panic in Anna's voice and spun on his heel, expecting her to tell him she'd twisted her ankle or, worse, had stepped on a snake.

'What?'

She stood next to the small shrub she'd ducked behind. Instead of answering, she pointed towards the horizon, back the way they'd walked.

In the distance, he could make out the tiny speck of the abandoned SUV, and his first instinct was to congratulate himself on how far they'd walked in such a short space of time.

And then he saw the dust cloud beyond that, bearing down on them at speed, the outline of vehicles silhouetted against the setting sun.

They were being pursued.

TWENTY-FOUR

'Shit.'

'How did they find us so easily?'

'They probably posted look-outs at that settlement,' said Dan. 'And other small towns around the border. They'd only need a couple of men at each, and then once someone calls it in, they can re-group.'

He pulled Anna to his side. 'Turn your back. Keep walking.'

'But they've got vehicles. We won't be able to out-run them.'

'No, but we *can* plan for what happens next. Hold this.' He passed his backpack over to her and pulled his mobile phone from his pocket, grateful the satellite signal was still relatively strong. He pressed the speed dial, and David Ludlow answered immediately.

'David, we're about to have company.'

'You think they'll take you hostage?'

Dan could hear the fear in the man's voice. Either the general's daughter would be killed or ransomed. The other alternatives didn't bear contemplating.

'Yes,' he said. 'But I don't intend to stick around, so do what you can.'

'We've got contacts in the Polisario,' said David. 'They haven't wanted to get involved yet – they might now that there's a direct threat on your lives. They've been taking pot-shots at Al Qaeda in the region for years, so I'll make some calls. If your pursuers take you hostage, how will I know where to send the Polisario?'

'Have you got my GPS coordinates from this call?'

'I have.'

'I'm going to leave my phone on. When they take us, hopefully you'll be able to track where we're going. Tell Mel to use the satellite to keep a look-out for it.'

'Copy that.'

'Thanks. Got to go.'

Dan ended the call, and deleted the call log and

numbers from its memory. He left it switched on and then bent down and removed the boot from his right foot.

He ripped out the insole, shoved the smartphone inside, and then slipped his boot back on.

Next, he pulled the Glock from his belt, removed the clip, and threw the components in different directions, far away from where he stood.

Anna watched him in disbelief. 'Dan? If they take us hostage, what are we going to do?'

'They won't believe I work in insurance if they find that on me,' he said.

He reached out and squeezed Anna's hand before retrieving his backpack from her. For someone unaccustomed to the situation, he was impressed by her ability to keep a level head and ask the right questions, but now sheer terror had taken over.

'Look around you,' he said. 'There's nothing for miles. Think about the houses we saw back there. I'm betting that wherever they take us, it'll be deserted, run-down.' He squinted up at the sky. 'There's only a few hours of daylight left, so nothing will happen tonight. We might get roughed up a bit, and they *will* intimidate you, but these people aren't in charge. They'll have a leader, but he's not going to be top dog. He'll be getting orders from someone else.'

'Same as Galal, you think?'

'Exactly.'

Anna looked over her shoulder. 'They're getting closer.'

'I know. I can hear them.'

'I'm scared, Dan.'

He stopped then, reached out, and gently tilted her chin until her eyes met his. 'I won't let them hurt you,' he said.

Anna swallowed, then wrapped her arms around him and buried her face in his chest. 'I just want to go home.'

'And I'll get you there.' He returned the hug. 'Be brave. I'll look after you.'

He heard the vehicles draw closer, the engines now accompanied by the baying of their pursuers.

Dan tilted his head until he could see them: three battered four-wheel drive vehicles, each carrying three men. Those who weren't driving were leaning out the windows, brandishing assault rifles.

Dan kept his face impassive as he watched them circle around where he and Anna stood.

The men were locals by the look of it, heavily armed but not professionally trained, evidenced by the way they waved their guns around instead of keeping them aimed at their quarry. No doubt the mercenary force was stretched to capacity over the region, smaller than he'd anticipated, and had employed local look-outs to bolster their presence.

He suppressed a smirk at a saying he'd heard once.

All piss and wind.

As in, all noise and no intent.

'Keep calm,' he murmured to Anna. 'They're doing this on purpose. Just do as they tell you, stay close, and you'll be fine. Remember, these men aren't in charge. They're acting on orders.'

'Okay,' she managed.

Dan held his hand up to his eyes and turned his head away from the dust cloud created by the vehicles as they continued to circle, the whooping cries of the men leaning out of the windows almost hysterical as they yelled in their unique dialect.

The driver of the lead vehicle stopped suddenly, causing the two following to skid to a halt, jolting the occupants from their seats before they righted themselves and sprang from the vehicles.

Dan crossed his fingers, hoping the men were simply over-excited and not on drugs as well. He could cope with stupidity and lack of training in his captors, but not if they were high on substances and unpredictable.

He forced his body into a non-threatening stance and raised his hands.

Anna copied him.

A stocky man led the others towards Dan and Anna.

Sunlight reflected off his sunglasses, his skin heavily wrinkled and tanned from years spent in the harsh desert environment.

He was slightly shorter than Dan, and he removed his sunglasses and squared his shoulders as he approached, his chin jutting upwards.

The leader cast his eyes over his men, waited until they were all watching him, and then strode from his vehicle and stood in front of Dan, who lowered his eyes.

The leader began to laugh, a deep guttural rumble that shook his shoulders. 'Ah, Mr Insurance Man. You will never cross this land on foot.' He lifted his chin and waved a hand in the direction of the abandoned SUV. 'And not in that.' He gestured towards his vehicles. 'Much better.'

'I'll bear that in mind next time, thanks,' said Dan. 'Are you here to give us a ride?'

The leader's face darkened, a moment before

he swung his weapon round and jabbed the butt viciously into Dan's stomach.

Dan's knees went out from under him as all the air was sucked from his lungs, and he heard Anna scream as he fell to the ground.

He leaned forward, his hands in the dirt as he concentrated on getting his breath back.

The leader bent down, grabbed the back of Dan's shirt and pushed him down until his face was touching sand and gravel, and hissed in his ear.

'You need to learn respect, Englishman.'

He straightened, and Dan raised his head a moment before two of the men grabbed his arms and forced him to his feet.

Dan staggered, his gut on fire, and glanced at Anna.

Her eyes wide, she struggled when two more of their attackers wrapped their hands around her arms, and Dan gave her an almost imperceptible shake of his head.

Don't fight them.

He couldn't explain that he'd had to demonstrate to the leader of the group that he wasn't a threat. By creating a situation where the leader of the group could exert his authority, he'd given the man the impression he had the upper hand.

'Bring their bags,' the leader commanded.

He snatched the backpacks from the men who retrieved them and tipped the contents of each onto the sand. His eyes lit up when he spotted the hard drive, and he held it up with a grin on his face.

'That's *mine*,' said Anna, trying to break free from the men who held her. 'Give it back.'

The leader's eyes darkened.

Dan clenched his fists.

With the hard drive in the militants' possession, only Anna could prevent them retrieving their money. He held onto the hope that they didn't suspect her of having the information they sought.

'Anna, leave it,' he murmured. He shook his head. 'It's not worth dying for.'

Anna stopped squirming, and they were dragged to the back seats of the first vehicle and their hands tied to the straps above the windows.

'Where are you taking us?' asked Dan. 'We're English and American citizens. We demand you take us to the proper authorities.'

The leader laughed and swept his hand expansively across the landscape. 'Here, *we* are the authorities, Mr Insurance Man.' He grinned, revealing blackened gums.

'Where are we going?' asked Anna, her voice shaking.

The man's gaze fell to her, and Dan gritted his teeth at the look in the man's eyes.

'You will be guests of our beloved leader tonight,' he said. 'In the morning, we will have a visitor. When he is finished with you, you will be mine.' He stepped forward and ran his fingers down Anna's cheek.

She flinched, and he grabbed her jaw, turning her head until their eyes met.

'You will be mine,' he repeated.

He stepped away from her, and the doors were slammed shut. The leader of the group climbed into the passenger seat and nodded at the driver, who set off in the direction Dan and Anna had been headed.

Dan cursed under his breath. He'd assumed the men would take them back to the settlement. Instead they were heading for unknown territory, and further into the desert.

He felt his mobile phone sticking into the sole of his foot and hoped the signal was still working.

And that the battery didn't run out before he had a chance to let David know where they were being taken.

TWENTY-FIVE

It took nearly an hour to reach the abandoned buildings the group were using as their base, the vehicle bouncing over the terrain on well-worn suspension.

Dan stole glances at their captors whenever he could.

The leader appeared on edge, despite his men's deference to him, and Dan couldn't work out if it was due to nerves or substance abuse. If it was the latter, it would make him unpredictable – and more dangerous.

The other men seemed almost nonchalant by comparison and reeked of marijuana.

Dan frowned as he turned away and watched

the sun set, the last of the orange and purple hues clouding the horizon.

The men who had captured them didn't display any of the qualities Dan had found in mercenaries he'd met over the years.

Their weapons handling was shoddy, for a start, and they appeared to be more of a local group of thugs than a highly trained and organised force.

Dan twisted his hands, testing the thin ropes that dug into his wrists. They held tight, and he rolled his shoulders, trying to alleviate the sensation of pins and needles in his arms.

He glanced across to Anna and raised an eyebrow.

She looked scared, but she nodded once and then continued to stare out the window next to her, the darkening desert stretching for miles beyond.

As the last of the sun's rays began to dip, the vehicle slowed, and Dan could see the outline of the derelict outpost.

The buildings looked as if they'd been constructed during the Spanish occupation – one that had ended decades ago; in places, walls had collapsed, leaving skeletal remains of supporting beams and broken roof tiles.

One building remained relatively intact, larger than the rest, and resembled a fort.

Dan sat up straighter as the vehicle approached it, assessing the layout as best he could from his restricted position.

Although run-down, it appeared to have been repaired using materials scavenged from the other buildings, and he admired the group's resourcefulness. They'd recognised the strength in the design of the small fort and had bolstered it rather than attempting to salvage the rest of the outlying ruins.

The four-wheel drive creaked to a halt, and the leader of the group and his driver climbed out.

Dan watched as a conversation ensued between them, the driver gesticulating and pointing at the fort until the leader appeared to acquiesce. The doors to the back seat were then ripped open, and Dan's hands were released from their bindings.

He rubbed his arms to get the circulation going again and checked to see that Anna was being untied as well. His arms were grabbed by the same two men who'd seized him before, and he was frog-marched towards a narrow opening in the fort wall.

'What is this place?' he asked, craning his neck to take in the height of the structure in the gloom.

'It is not your business,' the leader growled.

He pushed through a heavy wooden door and led the way into a narrow passageway.

Dan kept his face passive, but his eyes flickered left and right as he took in his surroundings.

He stumbled at the entrance to another room, the door open.

Inside, an array of weaponry littered the floor – crates with Russian markings on the side, rocket-propelled grenade launchers lined up against one wall, and boxes and boxes of ammunition.

His captors grabbed his arms and steadied him, dragging him into the depths of the building, but he'd seen enough.

Anna's fears about an organised uprising were real, and somehow he had to stop it.

TWENTY-SIX

Dan clenched his jaw as he was pushed over the threshold into a room to his right, moments before he heard Anna being dragged in after him.

A single candle burned brightly on a wooden table, the crooked surface of which appeared as if it had been nailed together by debris from the original fort.

The leader of the men who had captured them brushed past Dan and laid the hard drive he'd taken from Anna's backpack on the table, then stepped back and addressed the man who sat behind it, his dark eyes blazing as he glared at his new guests.

Although his skin was pock-marked by childhood disease and burned a deep brown by the sun, Dan reckoned him to be in his forties, no more.

Deep wrinkles creased his cheeks, and his headdress did little to disguise a receding hairline.

'They were caught trying to escape,' the man said. 'And that was in the woman's bag.'

'You have done well. This will be remembered.'

The militiaman bowed, then moved to the door and crossed his arms, his features giving nothing away.

The man behind the table rose from the chair and picked up the hard drive, turning it over in his hand.

'You know, Miss Collins, it would have been much easier if you had simply handed this over to the police.' His eyes flashed. 'Much easier.'

'Who are you?' asked Dan.

A round was chambered by one of the men behind him, the sound reverberating off the solid stone walls.

Dan automatically raised his hands in the air.

'I am Salim abd-al-Aziz,' the man said. 'And you are now mine.'

Dan kept his hands up. 'I demand you hand us over to our embassies in Rabat,' he said, his voice urgent. 'This is outrageous.'

Salim's eyes narrowed. 'It is not your place to negotiate, Mr Insurance Man,' he said, his voice dangerously low. 'I would remind you that you are in a very precarious position at the moment.'

For such a large man, he crossed the room with efficiency, before slamming his fist into Dan's stomach.

Dan dropped to the floor, the sound of Anna's scream reaching his subconscious as he struggled to breathe.

He screwed up his eyes, panting to try and counteract the burning sensation that fanned out through his body.

He raised himself to his hands and knees, seconds before Salim crouched down beside him and pulled one of Dan's ears, forcing him to the floor once more.

'I have what I need,' he hissed, and used his other hand to point at the hard drive on the table, and then to Anna. 'You are, as the Americans say, "surplus to requirements".'

Dan tried to ignore the pain at the side of his head. His vision blurred, and he saw Anna standing with her hands to her mouth, a look of sheer terror etched across her features.

Somehow, he needed get the militant leader to focus on him, not Anna, and keep them both alive until he could get her away from the fort.

'You can't kill me,' he said. 'I'm the only one who has the codes.'

Salim's hand dropped from Dan's ear, surprise in his eyes. His eyes flickered between Dan and Anna.

Dan held his breath.

Salim straightened. 'Is it true?' he asked Anna.

She nodded. 'I'm – I'm useless with computers.' She forced a nervous laugh. 'That's why I have to rely on the men to do that for me.' She shrugged. 'I can't access the money without him.'

Dan shot Anna a glance and stayed still, watching Salim's face as the man processed her words.

Finally, his attention fell upon Dan once more, and he sneered.

Dan had no time to react as Salim's foot lashed out and caught him under the chin.

His head snapped back, and he grunted as his skull met the wooden floor.

As he groaned, the militant stooped over him, lifted his arm, and removed the watch from his wrist.

'Get up,' he snarled.

Dan hissed through his teeth as fire tore through his belly and did as he was told. Instinctively, he edged closer to Anna before the man who held her dragged her backwards out of his reach.

Salim chuckled and wandered back to the table where Anna's hard drive lay. He ran his fingers over it before picking up the grenade next to it. A manic expression crossed his face as he returned to where Dan stood, tossing the grenade between his right and left hands.

'It would be a terrible waste if something *bad* were to happen to you before we could let you go,' he said.

'What do you mean?'

Salim turned to his men and laughed, the small group joining in, bolstering his ego.

Dan saw the man's stature increase at the reaction of his men and wondered where the conversation was headed.

He soon found out.

'Enough!' yelled Salim.

Dan took a step back.

In one fluid motion, Salim spun on his heel to face Dan once more, pulled the pin from the grenade, and tossed it to Dan.

He held up the pin and laughed.

'Fuck!'

Dan's eyes widened as his hands automatically

caught the grenade, his highly trained mind already counting the seconds.

Three or five?

Anna screamed.

Time slowed as he frantically sought a way out of the room to dispose of the small bomb. The single window was too narrow and too far away, and there was nowhere for him to run.

Salim's men had stopped laughing and were looking as scared as he felt, each of them backing away rapidly as he pushed past them, trying to find a way to get rid of the grenade in his hands.

Then he became aware of a wheezing sound from Salim's direction, and he pivoted to face the warlord, confusion swamping him.

A bellow emanated from the man's lungs, and he swung round to point at his men.

'Every time!'

They dutifully laughed, and Dan glanced down at the grenade in his hands.

'Bastard,' he murmured. He held it up so Anna could see. 'It's decommissioned,' he explained.

Salim approached, wagging his finger. 'You would be wise to hold your tongue in future, Mr Insurance Man. Next time, it might be real.'

Dan resisted the urge to throw the grenade at

the other man's forehead, fought down his rage, and instead dropped it into Salim's outstretched hand.

Anna ran to him, and he pulled her into a hug.

'It's okay.'

'He's a madman,' she whispered.

'Shh,' urged Dan.

He wholeheartedly agreed with the sentiment, but now wasn't the time to antagonise Salim further by pointing out his lack of social skills.

His attention snapped back to Salim as he called out to one of his men and threw the grenade at him.

The men in the room laughed, tossing the decommissioned weapon backwards and forwards until Salim held his hand up to stop the game.

'Enough.'

Salim placed the pin back in the grenade and stood for a moment, removing and replacing the pin as if lost in thought, before setting the grenade on the table next to him and turning his attention to the leader of the men who had captured Dan and Anna. 'Jamil, have your men take them to the cells.' He raked his eyes over Anna's body once more. 'Do not let your men near the woman. Not until I say so.'

He leered at her as she was led away, and Dan

clenched his fists as two men grabbed his arms and shoved him in the same direction.

As they reached the door, Salim's voice rang out.

'Wait.'

His men stopped, curious expressions on their faces.

Salim crossed the room and placed his hand on Dan's shoulder.

'Take off your right boot, Mr Insurance Man.'

Dan frowned. 'Why?'

'You appear to be limping,' said Salim. 'Yet, I did not strike your foot.'

Dan cursed under his breath.

Reluctantly, he removed his boot and held it out to Salim.

The militant leader smiled. 'Tip it upside down.'

Dan sighed but did as he was told.

The satellite phone clattered to the floor, and as Salim bent down to retrieve it, it was all Dan could do to stop himself from aiming a kick at the man's head.

Instead, he put his boot back on and met Salim's eyes as they both straightened.

A manic gleam stared back at him.

'Did you really think you could call for help?' the man sneered.

He cleared the space between them, wrenched Dan away from the men who held him, and dragged him to the small opening in the wall behind the table.

'Look,' he said, shoving Dan in the back. 'Look.'

Dan's eyes roamed the moonlit desert beyond the fort.

Not a single light shone in the distance; there were no other signs of civilisation.

He turned back to Salim and frowned.

'You may be thinking of a way to escape and get help,' said Salim. He pointed at the landscape. 'But you will never walk the desert beyond here.'

Dan saw the man's eyes glaze over but stayed silent.

'When I was a boy,' said Salim, 'the Moroccans dropped napalm and phosphorus on the people that lived south of their border. There are unexploded bombs that litter the earth all around here.' His eyes met Dan's. 'Have you ever seen what napalm or phosphorus does to a man's body, Mr Insurance Man?'

He pulled back the sleeves of his robes, unveiling skin destroyed by horrific burn scars.

'Some of us have never forgotten,' he said. He

turned and beckoned to his guards. 'Get them both out of my sight.'

As they were led through the interior of the fort towards a set of rooms that had had their doors torn off and replaced with metal bars as makeshift cells, he surveyed everything that lay around the space, knowing he had to get Anna as far away as possible.

With luck, David and Mel would have traced their GPS location, but Dan wouldn't take any chances.

Salim was certainly crazy, whether through illness or simply on the power he held over those around him.

Either way, he was proving to be unpredictable, and that made Dan more nervous.

TWENTY-SEVEN

Salim waited until Dan and Anna had been led away and then filled a cup with lukewarm water from a jug on the table and drank deeply.

He swallowed and pointed at Jamil. 'Contact the Russian,' he said. 'Tell him we have what he seeks.'

Jamil nodded and scuttled from the room, his footsteps receding in the confines of the passageway beyond.

Salim replaced the cup on the table and turned it between his fingers. In the candlelight, the moisture on the base of the vessel left circles on the wooden surface. Salim's eyes traced the patterns while he contemplated his next move.

The fort was easy to defend, and although it

was only three storeys high, over the past few months his men had blocked all entranceways save for the main doorway and a smaller one to the rear that was only used to restock provisions, and which remained bolted shut at all other times.

The stature of the building allowed an uninterrupted panoramic view of the surrounding landscape, ensuring no enemies could surprise the fort's occupants.

Salim's lips thinned.

The Spanish colonists' design would work to his advantage all these decades after their demise.

His hand moved to the Englishman's watch. Holding it up to the meagre light, he grunted in satisfaction. It appeared to be new, a latest model of a well-respected Swiss manufacturer that he'd seen on advertising billboards in the capital.

Salim slipped the strap around his wrist, admiring the workmanship of the timepiece.

'Spoils of war,' he murmured.

He frowned and peered closer at the time displayed on the watch face. It would be several hours before the Russian and his men would arrive.

Salim had told the truth to Dan – no-one attempted to cross the Western Saharan desert at night near the borders. Death caused by stumbling onto unexploded ordnance was a very real possibility.

Salim cocked his head to one side as another thought struck him.

That of the American woman currently held prisoner under his command.

He licked his lips.

Would she tell the Russian?

Would he care?

His top lip curled. In his heart, he knew the Russian would gouge his eyes out and have his balls if he touched the woman before the information had been extracted from her.

He clenched his fist and fought down the urges. His time would come.

Salim pulled out one of the wooden chairs next to the table and pushed his dirty robes out of the way as he sat.

Automatically, he reached out for the decommissioned grenade. A smile played across his lips as he withdrew the pin then replaced it, over and over, the pinch and release of metal on metal soothing his fraught nerves.

He straightened his shoulders and reached out for the cup of water, aware he had to remain calm in the eyes of his men, conscious of the fact he couldn't afford to look fearful or else show his weakness to them.

No, he resolved, he would obey the Russian's instructions.

He would remain loyal to the Russian's orders.

And he would claim the American woman as his own.

TWENTY-EIGHT

A key turned in the well-oiled lock, and the men who had brought Dan and Anna to the cells walked away, talking loudly, their voices and laughter gradually receding as they left the bowels of the fort.

Dan could imagine what they'd been discussing, and it angered him. He turned to see Anna backed up against the far wall of the room, her arms across her chest while she shivered uncontrollably.

In three strides, he'd cleared the space between them, reached out, and tilted her chin until her eyes met his.

'I won't let them harm you,' he said. 'Do you understand?'

A large tear escaped and ran down her left cheek, and he could feel her trembling under his touch.

'Hey,' he said, a little more forcefully. 'I mean it.'

'They're going to kill us,' she whispered. 'But they'll rape me first, won't they?'

Dan pulled her close and lowered his mouth to her ear. 'I'll get us out of here,' he murmured. 'Try to be brave.'

He straightened, and she frowned.

'How?'

He put a finger to his lips and then glanced over his shoulder at the sound of footsteps, closely followed by the stench of stale body odour.

One of the younger men had returned, his whole body posture suggesting he was less than pleased to be the one sent to guard the hostages. A cigarette dangled from the side of his mouth, and his beard was unkempt rather than being neatly trimmed as a sign of religious devotion.

His rifle slung over one shoulder, he approached the bars of the cell with his hands shoved into dirty tracksuit pants before removing the cigarette from his mouth and crushing it underfoot. He wiped his hands on a stained vest top with a logo on the front that depicted an American football team Dan felt confident the man had never supported, and leered at his prisoners.

Dan turned his back to the man and surveyed the cell.

The stink of excrement and urine still filled the damp air, and Dan was sure the stains nearby were blood.

He averted his eyes, not wishing Anna to pick up on his train of thought.

A window had been set high in the far wall, but this too was barred, and the stonework showed no sign of deterioration. Moonlight pooled through the narrow opening, helping to alleviate some of the shadows of the cell where light from the guard's lamp couldn't reach.

Dan guided Anna across to the far side of the cell, where they lowered themselves to the stone floor and sat with their backs to the wall, legs outstretched.

The guard tried to look nonchalant as he turned an old dilapidated chair towards himself and sat in it, his rifle cradled across his thighs as his hooded eyes contemplated the man and woman beyond the steel bars in front of him.

Dan lowered his gaze, brought his knees up to chest height, balanced his elbows on them, and closed his eyes.

'Are you sleeping?' said Anna, her tone incredulous.

'Shh,' said Dan out the side of his mouth. 'Copy me.'

He heard a faint sigh of exasperation but kept his eyes closed. He trusted her to do as she was told.

He also trusted his gut instinct that their young guard would soon drift off, bored by the monotony of guarding prisoners who were doing nothing more than sleeping.

While he waited, Dan recalled what he'd learned about the fort's inhabitants since their capture.

He'd neither seen nor heard any women apart from Anna, which meant the men were self-sufficient, cooking for themselves. He also guessed that the younger men had probably joined Salim on the promise of glory – yet were relegated to menial duties normally carried out by women.

Such tactics would breed resentment quickly, and Dan suspected some of Salim's men weren't as loyal as the warlord imagined.

They were certainly untrained, perhaps another feature of Salim's determination to rule with an iron grip – if his men were badly trained, they'd be less likely to stage an uprising against him.

He'd also neither seen nor heard any other men

in the building apart from those who had travelled in the three vehicles plus two who had emerged from the fort upon their arrival, so it was a small group, probably comprised of the most powerful man in the neighbourhood and his cronies, and no-one else.

Dan let his head drop a little and kept his eyes closed, his breathing steady.

Anna's head dropped to his shoulder, and she faked a small snore.

Dan fought the urge to smile, and instead his thoughts returned to escape.

Salim was evidently acting on orders, in all likelihood from the mercenary force whose weapons were being kept in the large room towards the entrance to the building. In which case, nothing would happen to Anna all the time Salim had to wait to be told what to do – and when.

So, Dan had less than twelve hours before Salim's superiors arrived at the fort.

He tried to concentrate, bottling down the fear that threatened to surface if he thought too hard about what Salim and his men would do to Anna if he failed.

The layout of the fort appeared to be basic: three floors built around a central stairway that was intersected by two passageways, one running east-west and the other north-south.

As they'd been led to the cell, Dan had craned his neck when they'd reached the stairway and had seen moonlight shining through the top of the roof. He guessed that the top floor was uninhabitable, most likely used by Salim's small group as a lookout post and nothing more.

He wondered if his phone signal had been strong enough that Mel could intercept it and pinpoint his location. If she had, then he hoped David's assertions that he could obtain help from the counter-terrorism unit of the Polisario army that patrolled the eastern reaches of the divided country were correct.

He frowned. Even if David could secure their help, he realised it'd be unlikely they'd reach the fort before Salim's masters.

He had to do something, and soon.

A loud snore from beyond the cell broke through his thoughts.

He opened one eye and checked the guard's position.

The man's head was tipped back, his mouth open, a trickle of spittle sliding down his jaw.

Dan nudged Anna and put his finger to his lips. 'Keep your voice down,' he whispered.

She nodded in response, her eyes darting to the sleeping guard, her lip curling in disgust.

Dan quietly got to his feet and padded across the floor to a crack between the boarded-up window. He peered through, angling his face until he could catch a glimpse of the stars above, wracking his memory for the observations he'd made the night before.

From memory, he figured the window faced north, and they'd travelled an hour at least before reaching it. He closed his eyes, trying to recall the map on his smartphone. At best guess, he figured they were still several hours from Mahbes, and certainly further away than they could expect to run or walk to freedom.

He opened his eyes and turned back to Anna, who watched him silently from her place on the floor. He wandered back to her, crouched, and bent down to her ear.

'I've got an idea. Do you trust me?'

TWENTY-NINE

Laughter filtered along the corridor towards the cells from the rooms the militants occupied, and Dan raised his gaze to their guard.

The man snuffled in his sleep, then began to snore once more, oblivious to his surroundings.

Dan sniffed the air and caught the familiar scent of marijuana wafting through the building.

His heart skipped a beat. If Salim's men were relaxed enough to trust the young guard to keep an eye on their prisoners while they in turn got stoned, it worked to his advantage. Out of all of the men he'd seen in the building, Salim was the only one who gave him cause for concern, and his plan had to work if he and Anna were to escape before daybreak.

'Okay, listen,' he murmured. 'We're going to have one shot at this, so we have to make it work.'

He laid out his plan to Anna, whose eyes grew wider as he set out what she needed to do. When he finished, he held her gaze and raised an eyebrow. 'Got all that?'

She didn't answer. Instead, her eyes darted to the man in the chair outside the cell and back to Dan.

'What if it doesn't work?' she hissed.

'Anna,' said Dan patiently, 'we need to get out of here tonight. Tomorrow, whoever is giving Salim orders will turn up, and we won't stand a chance.' His voice softened. 'If I'm going to get you away from here, alive, then we need to do this *now*, understand?'

She swallowed, stole another glance at the guard, and then turned back to Dan. 'Okay. Let's do it.'

He reached out and squeezed her shoulder. 'Good girl.'

He rose to his full height and cricked his back muscles, all the time keeping an eye on the sleeping guard while Anna scooped up the blankets, gathering them together.

He glanced down. 'Ready?'

'Yes.'

He nodded, then strode towards the bars of the cell and blew a low whistle.

The guard's eyes twitched but remained closed.

'Oi,' said Dan, careful to keep his voice low. 'Hey.'

The guard mumbled in his sleep, then one of his arms fell to his side, and he began to snore once more.

Dan exhaled, exasperated. He turned and stalked around the small room, then found some plaster chips that had fallen away from one of the walls and carried them over to the barred door.

'Hey,' he said again, and threw half the chips at the guard.

They showered him in fine gravel and dust, peppering his head and shoulders.

The guard's eyes opened immediately, wide and staring as he appeared to try to get his bearings, and then he glared at Dan and stood up.

Dan beckoned to him. 'Get over here.' He jerked his thumb over his shoulder. 'She's not feeling well.'

Anna groaned and sounded so convincing that Dan checked to make sure she was really acting. She caught his eye, then let out another theatrical groan and clutched her stomach.

Dan turned his attention back to the guard.

'Listen, I think it's something she ate.' He mimed eating and then rubbed his stomach, hoping to hell the guard took the hint.

The man frowned, took two steps forward, and then stopped, confusion clouding his features.

Dan beckoned to him. 'Hurry, man. I don't know what to do.' He knew the man couldn't understand him, so he made his tone urgent, pleading, and tried to look as worried as possible. He checked Anna's position as the man drew closer, then spun round as the guard reached the iron bars, threaded his hand through the gap, seized the man's vest top, and pulled.

Hard.

The man over-balanced, arms flailing, and a dull *thunk* resonated around the small space as his skull met the metalwork.

Dan loosened his grip as the man fell back, dazed.

He frowned.

The man was still conscious.

Dan yanked at the man's clothes again.

Harder.

This time, the man collapsed the moment his head met the iron bars, and Dan felt him sag under his grip.

'Now!' Dan hissed.

Anna ran across the room and began searching the pockets of the guard's tracksuit pants while Dan held him aloft.

'Got them,' she said a few moments later, and extracted a set of two keys.

'Get the door open,' said Dan. 'Hurry.'

He could feel the guard's deadweight beginning to slip from his grip. He thrust out his other hand and steadied the man while Anna fumbled with the keys, trying to find the lock on the opposite side of the cell grille.

The steel bars were designed to swing outwards, and if Dan dropped the guard's body before Anna could release the door, they'd be trapped, the man's body blocking the door.

After what seemed like an age, Anna managed to insert the right key, and the grille shifted under their combined weight.

'Go,' said Dan. 'Push it open.'

Between them, they opened the grille, and Dan pushed past Anna and grabbed the guard under his arms.

Blood trickled from a gash behind the man's left ear, and Dan made sure none of it fell to the floor as he dragged the man into the cell and pulled him across to the darkened far side of the room.

'Help me,' said Dan.

He bunched up the man's body into a foetal position, his back to the cell opening, and took one of the blankets Anna held out to him.

'What if he wakes up?' whispered Anna.

Dan reached out to check the man's pulse and shook his head. 'I don't think he's going to wake up any time soon,' he said. 'His pulse is too weak.'

He straightened and dashed towards the open door. 'Stay here,' he said.

'What? Wait.' Anna ran to the grille as Dan swung the door shut, desperation in her eyes. 'Don't leave me.'

Dan reached out and grasped her fingers. 'You have to stay here. Curl up on the other blanket in front of the guard. Hide him from view with your body. If anyone comes here, it has to look as if the guard has left his post of his own accord, and that we're both in there asleep.'

He turned and picked up the rifle the guard had dropped and checked the breach. It was clogged with dirt and grease, and Dan's nose wrinkled in disgust. He emptied the rounds, put them in his pocket, and propped the now useless weapon against the wall.

'Back in a minute,' he said.

'Where are you going?'

'There's a weapons cache near the entrance

they brought us through. I'm going to get us out of here.' He squeezed her hands and let go. 'And I want to take out as many of the guards as I can before we go. Otherwise we're just going to end up with them all on our tail again.'

Anna nodded, understanding. 'Be careful, okay?'

Dan winked. 'I'll be back. Don't wait up.'

THIRTY

Dan padded away from the cells and edged along the far wall of the corridor, keeping his profile in the shadows.

A whirring mechanical noise emanated beyond an outer wall, while next to him candles had been placed in cavities dug into the wall, casting a dull light, and Dan realised that any power to the building would be from a diesel-powered generator. As he progressed along the passageway, he leaned across and blew out some of the candles, reducing visibility to a minimum.

He sniffed.

Someone, somewhere in the building, was cooking, and the fragrant aroma of spices and meat cut through the stagnant air.

The passageway widened, and the first of two doors were revealed. Dan wanted to explore, to get his bearings and work out where their captors were, but first he had to find a weapon.

He slipped past the doors after checking the way was clear and made his way through the rabbit-warren of corridors towards the arms cache he'd seen.

The sound of muted conversation and the occasional laugh reached his ears, and he realised that with the guard on duty in the cells, the rest of the men were relaxing. With food in their bellies and marijuana in their lungs, they'd be unaware of his movements.

He didn't trust Salim though; the leader of the motley bunch of militants had already shown his sociopathic tendencies and would likely ignore any temptation to take recreational drugs in front of his men – especially with the likelihood of his paymasters arriving the following day.

He recalled that the passageway intersected with another at what he supposed was the mid-point of the fort; when he and Anna had been taken to the cells, they'd headed straight across the path of the other stone-hewn corridor, and he hadn't had a chance to see what lay down either of the other passageways before his captors had pushed him onwards.

Now, he slowed his pace further as he approached the junction, the voices of the men filtering from the passageway to his left. He checked the way in front of his position to ensure it was clear, then to the right. Once satisfied no-one would find him on the loose, he edged around the corner to try to see where the noise was coming from.

A glow emanated from the end; firelight flickered over the walls, reflected from an open doorway to another room. Swirls of marijuana-fuelled smoke escaped into the passageway, twisting as they filtered towards the exposed beams that had once held a ceiling aloft, and Dan realised that the men were in the old kitchen area of the fort.

Laughter and cat-calling filled the space, together with the sounds of plates being scraped across a hard surface and the occasional loud belch.

He froze when Salim's voice cut through the rest, his tone argumentative, the guttural tones of his native dialect echoing off the walls.

A silence followed his words, the only sound coming from a log that crackled loudly in the fire, and then one of the men guffawed, the rest joined in, and the moment passed.

Dan exhaled, letting some of the pressure that had built up in his chest to pass. Satisfied the men were going to be occupied for a while yet, Dan hurried across the intersection and back the way he'd been brought earlier that evening.

He soon drew level with the door to the room Salim had occupied, the table inside illuminated by a single candle. Dan's mouth twitched as he ran his eyes over the contents of the table, and a refinement to his original plan began to form in his mind.

Taking a spare candle from the table, he lit it, then quickly exited the room, turned left, and finally rounded the corner to where he'd seen the guns and ammunition.

He left the candle on the floor just inside the door to avoid it falling over near any of the munitions crates and began to rummage through the contents of the wooden boxes.

Pushing the packing material aside, he soon pulled out two Russian-made pistols and an assault rifle, then turned to the other side of the room and pocketed as much ammunition as he could carry.

Finally, he crouched down next to a single box he'd spotted near the door, picked out one of the objects that lay inside, and tossed it in his hand, testing its weight, his heartbeat racing.

An idea struck him, and he grabbed a second grenade.

He snuffed out the candle, pulled the door until it was almost closed, and removed the pin from the first grenade. Sweat poured from his brow as he kept his thumb on the safety lever and wrapped the crude tripwire around it.

The trap set, he hurried back to Salim's room, keeping his footsteps light on the stone floor.

Entering the space, he put the candle back where he'd found it, then reached out and picked up Salim's decommissioned grenade.

He held it up next to the one he'd taken from the munitions room, turning them in the light from the candle that still flickered on Salim's table.

They were identical.

THIRTY-ONE

Dan returned to the cell without incident and passed one of the guns to Anna before pulling the grille across the doorway.

'Nothing happened. What did you do?'

'Patience,' and Dan. 'You'll find out soon enough.'

'What do we do now?' asked Anna.

'We wait,' said Dan.

A loud groan emanated from the corner of the room where the guard lay.

Dan wandered over to the curled-up form, crouched down, and checked the man's pulse. It was still weak, but Dan reached out, tore a strip from the blanket, and tied the man's hands behind him before placing a gag over his mouth in case he awoke and cried out, alerting the others.

'These guns are brand new,' said Anna as Dan returned to his position at the door. She turned the weapon in her hands before she fed the ammunition Dan held out to her into the magazine.

'At least you know you were right about what the money was being used for,' said Dan.

'Great,' muttered Anna under her breath. She sighted the gun across the room, then relaxed her grip and eyed the passageway beyond the cells. 'Why don't we go now? You made it to Salim's room and back without being seen. We could leave.'

Dan shook his head. 'They'll have a couple of look-outs on the roof as a minimum,' he said. 'At least, I would if I were Salim.'

Anna wrinkled her nose. 'He's the only one who seems to know what he's doing,' she said. 'The rest—'

'Would be dangerous if we provoked them,' said Dan. 'They're thugs.'

Dan automatically raised his wrist and then cursed as he remembered Salim had removed his watch. He had no idea how long it would take for his plan to take effect, but he hoped to be on the move under cover of darkness. The longer they waited, the more tired they would become, especially Anna who was unused to combat situations.

He stole a glance at the woman next to him. He hardly recognised the scrawny twenty-something he'd met when she was still a university student. Now, she was more mature and self-assured, despite the trauma she'd endured the past two days.

She held the gun in her hand with ease, and with the general as her father, he had no doubt about her marksmanship.

He fleetingly wondered, though, if she would shoot another person, even if her life depended on it.

His thoughts were interrupted by noise from the men's quarters.

'They're coming,' hissed Anna, her body tensing next to his.

'Stay here,' said Dan under his breath. 'Don't fire unless I tell you.'

The scraping of a chair being moved reached his ears, and then footsteps echoed along the passageway.

In his mind, Dan envisaged the small group disbanding after their meal, splitting up through the fort to sleep or carry out whatever duties Salim had set them.

He figured one man would be sent to relieve their guard from his post.

'When he appears, distract him,' said Dan. 'Make sure he looks at you.'

Dan pushed the cell door open and hurried over to the opposite wall, where he'd be out of sight from the guard until he walked into the room.

Anna ran to the cell door as the footsteps grew louder.

'Hello?' she called. 'Please – help me. I think there's something wrong. Hurry!'

The footsteps quickened, and Anna reached out through the bars of the cell.

Dan could sense the guard's presence, heavy breathing reaching his ears a split second before the man's form filled the doorway.

Dan didn't hesitate. He spun away from the wall, dragged the man into the room, and forced him to the floor in a headlock, using the guard's own momentum to drive him into the hard stonework.

The man's body went limp on impact under Dan's weight, his head lolling to one side at an impossible angle.

Dan pushed himself upright, checked the man's pulse, and then shook his head.

'Okay,' he said over his shoulder. 'Let's go.'

The sound of sobbing reached his ears, and he

looked up to see Anna trying to regain her composure.

He stood, tore open the cell door, and pulled her into his arms.

'We need to go,' he said.

'Sorry,' said Anna. 'It's just – I've never seen you like that.' She sniffed. 'That was scary.'

'It was him or us,' said Dan patiently. 'Come on. Pull it together,' he added. 'We're not out of danger yet.'

She wiped her eyes and nodded.

At that moment, an explosion ripped through the building, and Dan reached out to steady Anna as the floor shook.

Parts of the wall next to them crumbled, and plaster dust rained from the ceiling as the noise died away, and the sound of screams and shouting filtered through the fort.

Anna's eyes widened. 'What the hell was that?'

Dan winked. 'The warranty ran out on Salim's toy grenade.'

THIRTY-TWO

'Go!'

Dan checked none of the militiamen were present, and pushed Anna through the door.

He began to follow, then pivoted and ran back to the cell, crouched down next to the unconscious guard and tore more strips from the blanket next to him.

He joined Anna, swung the door shut, and shouldered the rifle.

'Here,' he said, and handed her one of the cloth strips. 'Tie this around your mouth and nose.' He waited until she was ready, and then grabbed her hand.

'Stay behind me. Do what I do. Watch our rear,' he commanded. 'Got it?'

She nodded. 'Got it,' she said, her voice muffled behind the cloth.

Confused shouting filtered along the passageway as they hurried towards their escape, the sound of a man's screams piercing the smoke-filled air.

Miraculously, candles still burned in some of the recesses, and Dan pulled down his makeshift mask to blow them out, casting their position into shadows.

He put a finger to his lips and turned as footsteps drew closer.

A curse echoed around the space, and Dan heard the distinct sound of a round being chambered. He clenched his jaw, forcing himself to wait until the last minute to show his position.

He signalled to Anna to crouch and stay down. He figured the guard would expect them to walk around the corner of the passageway.

Instead, Dan crept forward in a stooped position, his rifle raised.

The guard spotted him a moment too late, and Dan fired a short burst as the man's finger found the trigger of his own weapon.

Dan threw himself to the floor as a hail of bullets hit the wall next to him, before the man fell to the ground, the gun silent.

'Okay, come on.' Dan straightened and beckoned to Anna. 'Let's find the back door to this place.'

Then a second explosion rocked the building, and Dan pulled Anna to the wall with him, shielding her face from the rush of air that was sucked from the passageway to fuel the flames.

'What–'

Anna's confused eyes found his.

'I also booby-trapped the arms cache,' said Dan. 'Let's go.'

He had realised when he'd planted the two live grenades that there was a risk of fire spreading uncontrollably once it exploded, but he was desperate. He had to get Anna away from the fort before reinforcements arrived in the morning.

Reaching the main passageway that bisected the fort, he turned the opposite way from where he'd found the arms cache, the air filled with choking smoke.

Breaking into a jog, he led the way to where he'd heard the sounds and aromas of cooking only hours before.

He slowed as they reached the room, signalled to Anna to stay behind him, then swung into the room, rifle raised.

The room was deserted, all its occupants having left to find the cause of the first explosion and arm themselves.

'Come on,' he said.

The back door to the fort was unguarded, another sign of the rag-tag militants' inexperience.

A single long piece of timber acted as a lock, and Dan slung his rifle over his shoulder.

He removed the timber, propped it against the wall, and then opened the door a crack, the rifle ready.

'Okay, we're clear,' he said, pushing the door open. 'Let's go.'

He waited until she was through, and then pushed the door shut, wedging a stone into the uneven surface of the frame to jam it.

He grabbed Anna's hand and pulled her towards the vehicles that were parked at the side of the building.

Dan tore open the door to the vehicle they'd travelled in to the fort and checked the ignition. He swore.

'What's the problem?'

'No keys.' He pointed towards another vehicle. 'Let's try that one.'

'Can't you hot wire this one?'

Dan glanced over the top of her head towards the fort. Angry shouts began to draw closer from the building, and then a heavy object was launched at the barricaded door.

It shook in its frame, but held, dust crumbling around its edges.

'No time,' said Dan. 'I don't think that door is going to hold for much longer.'

He grabbed Anna's hand and they ran towards the other vehicle, Dan breathing a sigh of relief as the firelight from the fort shone upon a single key in the ignition.

He turned, aimed the stolen rifle at the other vehicles and shot out the tyres, then slid behind the wheel and started the engine, the sound of urgent voices reaching his position as another resounding crash reverberated against the thick wooden doors of the fort.

'Use your gun to smash the brake lights,' he yelled as Anna opened the passenger door.

She nodded and disappeared to the rear of the vehicle, then returned and slammed her door shut moments before Dan released the hand-brake, took his bearings from the compass that bobbed on the dashboard, and floored the accelerator.

He pushed the assault rifle towards Anna.

'Take this. If anyone comes out that door while you can still take a shot, do it.'

'What about the unexploded bombs Salim told us about?'

Dan peered into the darkness. 'I'd rather take my chances with those than wait for the Russians to arrive.' His eyes found hers. 'Wouldn't you?'

'Yes.' She wound down her window and twisted in her seat until she had a clear view.

Dan's eyes flickered to the fuel gauge.

Half full.

He swore again.

'What?' Anna peered over her shoulder at him.

'We've only got half a tank of fuel.'

'It's okay,' she said, raising her voice over the sound of the wind rushing through her window. 'There's a jerry can on the back of the vehicle. I think it's full.'

For one moment, Dan thanked his stars for the good luck, and then realised that if Salim's men got one clear shot at the rear of the vehicle, he and Anna were sitting on a potential bomb.

'Crap,' he muttered. 'Could this week get any worse?'

He changed through the gears and flicked the headlights onto low beam, checking the mirrors at the same time Anna cried out.

'They're coming!'

'Short bursts,' he commanded. 'Don't waste the ammunition. The best you can do from here is provide cover fire until we get out of their range.'

Anna shuffled around until her back was pressed against the dashboard and planted her feet against the back of her seat. Wedged into place, she raised the rifle and pulled the stock into the muscle between her arm and her breast to counteract the recoil.

Dan swung the vehicle so Anna could take aim.

No sooner had he spun the wheel than the noise of gunfire filled the four-wheel drive as Anna let loose a volley of rounds, her face a mask of concentration, her ponytail whipping across her forehead. She paused and readjusted her grip.

'Can you turn to your right a bit?' she yelled.

Dan glanced across, noted her range, and made a slight correction in the direction he drove, angling the vehicle so Anna now had the door to the fort almost directly in front of her.

'Got you.' Anna's chin dropped as her eyes found her targets, and she pulled the trigger again. The staccato burst of energy stopped as quickly as it had started. 'I think I got two of them.'

'Good,' said Dan. 'Are the rest taking cover yet?'

'Yes.'

Dan didn't wait for further confirmation. He reached across and dragged Anna back into the vehicle. 'Wind the window up,' he said. 'That's enough. We're far enough away now.'

He floored the accelerator and pointed the four-wheel drive into the night.

THIRTY-THREE

Dan flipped the windscreen visor into place and angled his head to avoid the worst of the sun's glare.

They'd driven without stopping for three hours, and the combination of heat, bright sunlight, and lack of water was beginning to take its toll on Dan's concentration.

As the pre-dawn light had begun to bathe the barren land, Dan had realised how lucky they'd been to escape when they did. Without his wristwatch, he'd lost track of time at Salim's fort. A shiver crawled across his shoulders at the thought that if Salim had never pulled the pin on the grenade, they could very well still be trapped there, awaiting their fate at the hands of the militant's paymasters.

Anna had collapsed into a fitful sleep over an hour ago, sheer exhaustion consuming her small frame.

Dan glanced across at her; she'd curled herself into the passenger seat, dust covering her eyelashes and a smear of blood on her cheek that she'd evidently wiped from a scratch that creased the bridge of her nose.

He swallowed. He couldn't even recall that she'd cried out in pain, and guilt washed over him. He'd simply assumed that she'd keep up, do as she was told, and aid him in their escape.

And she had done so, without complaint.

He blinked and realised that for the first time ever, by deliberately killing first the guard and then Salim, he'd chosen to take a life rather than try to find a solution that avoided that outcome. And then, he wondered when he had changed.

He shook his head to clear the thought.

They'd passed no-one in their haste to put some distance between themselves and the rag-tag remainder of Salim's men. Dan had deliberately avoided well-worn tracks, not wishing to stumble into the very people they were trying to evade.

Instead, he'd taken a convoluted route while keeping a steady eye on the compass. Not that he trusted it explicitly. Twice he'd smacked the plastic globe on the dashboard with the heel of his hand, convinced it was showing him the wrong reading. As a precaution, he'd taken regular note of the sun's position as it rose higher into the sky.

He squinted, trying to ignore the pounding headache above his right eyebrow.

A light on the dashboard flashed at the same time an electronic *ping* filled the vehicle.

'What was that?' Anna stirred in her sleep, stared wide-eyed at the empty horizon that spread for miles around them as if she'd momentarily forgotten where she was, and then leaned across.

'Fuel gauge,' said Dan, and slowed the vehicle to a standstill. He unclipped his seatbelt. 'Time to find out how much is really in that jerry can.'

He pulled the lever under the steering column, then jumped out of the vehicle and let out an involuntary grunt when his boots found dirt. Cramp shot up one leg, and he swore under his breath as he limped towards the back of the vehicle and tried to ease out the cricks from his muscles.

'Are you okay?'

'Yeah.'

Anna joined him at the rear of the vehicle, her brow creasing. 'Are you sure?'

He winked. 'Wouldn't miss this for the world.'

Despite everything, she managed a small smile.

Dan unclipped the bindings that criss-crossed the jerry can and lifted it off the metal bracket that had been crudely welded to the back of the vehicle, testing its weight as he carried it round to the fuel cap.

'We might be in luck.'

'Is it full?' Anna traipsed behind him, retying her ponytail.

'No, but better than I thought.'

He hefted the plastic container against the side of the vehicle and unscrewed the cap, the fumes wafting on the hot air making him slightly light-headed. He turned his head and began to pour.

'I need to pee. Back in a minute,' said Anna.

'Okay.'

He glanced up and followed her progress round the other side of the vehicle, then lowered his gaze and concentrated on emptying the jerry can.

By his calculations, there were about twenty litres of fuel left, which should last them another hundred miles, allowing for evaporation.

He hoped.

His stomach rumbled, and he realised he was running on empty, his last proper meal having been on the flight from Essaouria. He ignored it; he'd eat when he could relax, or the opportunity arose. Not before. He cleared his throat and hawked onto the dirt next to his feet.

Emptying the jerry can, he recapped the lid and refastened it onto the back of the vehicle.

'Dan? There are vehicles coming this way.'

Anna reappeared, her eyes wide, and pointed towards a dust cloud bearing down on them from the eastern horizon.

Dan pulled the last rope to secure the jerry can, folded his arms across his chest, and squinted at her. 'You've got to stop doing that.'

'What?'

'Every time you take a piss, someone turns up.'

He brushed past her, squeezing her arm to let her know he was joking, and leant into the vehicle.

He reached out and swept the assault rifle and hand gun out of sight, keeping them within easy reach of the door in case he needed them, then pushed the door until it sat in the frame, resting on the latch.

'What do we do?' Anna appeared at his side.

'Wait and see,' he said.

They shaded their eyes from the sun and watched; as the dust cloud grew closer, two vehicles appeared, large forms that bore down on them.

'Those don't look like four-wheel drives,' said Anna.

'They're military.'

'Military?'

'Yeah.' Dan dropped his hand from his brow.

'The Russians?'

The vehicles ground to a halt only metres away from them.

'No,' said Dan. 'Polisario. Stay here.'

He waited until the passenger door of one of the armoured personnel carriers opened, then began to walk towards it, his hands held up.

A man lowered himself onto the ground, closely followed by four soldiers who dropped from the rear of the truck. As one, they raised their weapons in Dan's direction.

'Crap,' he muttered. He cleared his throat. 'I'm English. Does anyone speak English?'

'What are you doing here?' The man who had climbed from the front of the vehicle held his hand up, and the four armed soldiers stopped in their tracks.

'We're trying to get to Mahbes,' said Dan. 'We were taken hostage.' He pointed over his shoulder. 'There were some men. In a fort. That way. We managed to escape.'

The man, who Dan assumed to be the commanding officer, turned to his men and gestured to them to lower their weapons. Once satisfied they weren't going to shoot Dan by accident, he stalked across the sand towards Dan, his eyes shaded by the peaked cap that he wore.

'Who are you?' he demanded.

'My name is Dan Taylor. I'm English. The lady by the vehicle is an American by the name of Anna Collins,' said Dan. 'We were taken hostage by someone named Salim abd-al-Aziz. We managed to escape a few hours ago.' He lowered his gaze and concentrated on looking contrite. 'We're trying to get to Mahbes. We need to leave the country.' He lifted his chin and met the commanding officer's eyes. 'Can you help?'

The man removed the sunglasses from his eyes. 'Maybe.'

Dan sighed. 'Look, we have no money. Everything we had was stolen. I'm just trying to get her to the border. She's been through hell.'

The commanding officer's eyes travelled from Dan to where Anna stood.

Dan resisted the urge to turn around. He knew how pitiful Anna looked, despite the brave face she'd put on when the vehicles had stopped.

The army officer took a step back and scratched his ear. 'Have you seen anyone else, apart from the men you describe?'

Dan shook his head and frowned. 'No. Who are you looking for?'

The man's jaw clenched, his eyes darting to the vehicle behind Dan. 'Some Russians,' he said. 'Are you sure?'

'I'm sure. There's no-one else around for miles. We've been driving for hours and haven't seen a soul.'

'Can you tell me about the fort?' asked the man, tilting his head to gauge Dan's reaction.

Dan realised David and Mel's message must've reached the right people. Somehow, before Salim had discovered Dan's phone, they'd got a lock on his position.

'You might find the men you're looking for there, I suppose,' he said, and shrugged. 'But they weren't there when we were.'

The officer grunted in response, then sighed and waved his hand. 'Mahbes is another hour in that direction.'

Dan swallowed. He'd been several degrees off course. He silently cursed the vehicle's malfunctioning compass and his own exhaustion. 'Thank you,' he managed.

The Sahrawi chuckled. 'Don't thank me,' he laughed. 'At least this way you stand a chance of getting to Mahbes before nightfall, and I don't have to waste time trying to locate your bodies for your embassies.'

He turned on his heel and stalked back to the armoured trucks, barking orders at his men.

Dan waited until they'd lowered their weapons and scurried towards the vehicles before returning to the four-wheel drive.

'What did he say?' asked Anna as he neared.

'They're trying to find some Russians,' he said.

'The ones who we're trying to stop?' Anna's voice went up a notch.

Dan held up his hand. 'Yes,' he said, trying to soothe her. 'The good news is, Mahbes is only an hour away.'

Anna's shoulders visibly sagged. 'Thank goodness,' she breathed. Her eyes opened wider. 'He's trying to tell us something.'

Dan swivelled on his toes, wondering what was going on.

He exhaled with relief when he saw the army officer waving to them, and then the man pointed to one of his soldiers, who was walking towards Dan and Anna, carrying what appeared to be a heavy jerry can.

'Extra fuel.' Dan shook his head in wonderment and hurried to meet the soldier halfway.

'Thank you,' he said. 'Thank you very much.'

It was evident the man didn't understand the words, but he smiled and bowed a little at the tone of Dan's voice, then jogged back to where his commanding officer stood waiting.

Dan held up his hand in farewell, then carried the fuel can back to the four-wheel drive.

He unclipped the empty can, threw it to the dirt, and fixed the full one in its place, gripping its sides and shaking it to make sure it held firm.

As he finished, the two army vehicles roared past, dust devils spinning in their wake, before quickly disappearing from view.

Dan hoped to hell they found their quarry, and fast.

'All right,' he said. 'Let's go.'

'Are we safe?'

Dan's eyes flickered in the blazing sunlight as he sought out the exact location the army officer had pointed to on the horizon. 'For now.'

THIRTY-FOUR

Gregori Abramov dropped his cigarette to the sand and ground it out with the heel of his boot.

The sun had begun to rise an hour after they'd reached the smouldering ruin of the fort, the stench of burnt flesh pervading Abramov's senses as he'd stepped from the lead vehicle.

His men had searched as best they could, careful not to brush against the broken walls of the building for fear of causing the rest of it to collapse on top of them, hunting for survivors.

Abramov pinched the bridge of his nose. Somehow, he didn't think the so-called insurance man had been responsible for so many deaths. No doubt those who were left had cut their losses and returned to their villages, eager to put as much distance between themselves and the fort as they could before he'd turned up.

He'd known it had been a risk agreeing to work with Galal to engineer the uprising, but his client had been insistent.

Very insistent.

Abramov's skin crawled as he thought of his thirteen-year-old daughter. As soon as he'd heard the client had terminated the contract with his predecessor and was likely to contact him, he'd ordered two of his men to kidnap the girl from his estranged wife under cover of darkness and spirit her out of the country. Even he didn't know where she'd been taken. It was safer for her that way.

Unfortunately, the client had a long reach, and he knew if he failed, then his daughter would be hunted down and used in order to make an example of him.

The client only dealt out contract work that yielded results or the contractor's death.

Abramov cursed his bad luck. It was his own fault the client had sought him out – he had a proven track record of fundraising for several successful coups around the world, bettered only by the Americans and their government's habit of trying to influence political agendas. He'd been too good, though, and now the client had him backed into a corner, unable to escape.

He had no doubt that the success of this current mission would lead to more work, always with the threat of the wellbeing of his daughter hanging over his head.

He snapped himself out from the thoughts tumbling through his mind as one of his men approached.

'Well?'

The man shook his head. 'There are two men on the ground on the other side of the building. Both badly burned. One was barely alive, so we dealt with him. You might want to try to talk to the other one.'

Abramov grunted. He'd heard the gunshot from where he'd been standing.

He trudged after the mercenary, keen to glean any information that would lead to the capture of the woman.

When he rounded the corner of the still smouldering building, he saw two of his men standing beside the badly burned form of a man on the ground.

'Please,' he begged, raising his hand up to Abramov as he approached. 'Have mercy.'

Abramov snorted. Mercy was something he held in short supply. He crouched, his arms resting on his knees as he surveyed the man's injuries with a practiced eye.

The burns to his skin were extensive, the thin man-made fibre of his trousers having melted into his legs whilst the tattered remains of his cotton shirt clung to his shoulders. One side of his head was unrecognisable, his ear shrivelled into his skull. His breath rasped from his exposed chest while his hands clawed at the air, his eyes wide and frightened.

Abramov's lips thinned.

He pulled his gun from his belt loop and held it up in front of the man's face. 'Is this what you want?'

The man nodded, desperation in his eyes.

Abramov leaned forward, baring his teeth, and pushed the barrel of the gun into the man's leg.

The militant arched his back and screamed, a primal cry of pain and anguish that reverberated off the stone walls that remained.

Abramov eased the pressure but kept the gun within sight of the man's eyes.

'What happened?'

The man panted, trying to force air into his smoke-damaged lungs. 'Jamil brought a man and a woman here,' he gasped. 'The man destroyed the fort. Salim is dead. Everyone is dead.'

'Where are the man and woman? Are they dead, too?'

'The man stole a vehicle. That's all I know.' The man's eyes pleaded with Abramov. 'Please. That's all I know.'

Abramov sighed, then straightened and dusted off his jeans before he stared out across the landscape. 'Shit.'

He raised his gun, aimed it at the militant, and pulled the trigger, a single blast that shattered the man's skull in an instant.

One of Abramov's men standing nearby raised an eyebrow. 'I didn't take you for being so sympathetic to another man's suffering.'

Abramov shot him a withering stare. 'I didn't do it to put him out of his misery,' he said. 'I did it so he wouldn't give the information to anyone else trying to follow us.' He turned to the man next to him. 'Was there anything else?'

'No. We found the location where the fire began – looks like an explosion started it, then the fire took hold and reached the arms cache. There's nothing left.'

'Shit.' Abramov spun on his heel and ran a hand over his cropped hair.

The fact that Salim had been stupid enough to keep all the weapons and ammunition together was bad enough, but for him to then store it in the same building he was using as accommodation for his men astounded the Russian.

He stared at the smudged haze on the horizon, knowing the smoke from the fire would have been seen for miles and that his time there was running out.

'We're leaving,' he shouted to his men, and waved his hand towards the vehicles.

'What now?' asked the man next to him.

'We find the girl,' said Abramov.

'Why? Shouldn't we put as much distance between ourselves and this place as possible? What use will it do trying to find her now?'

'Because the bitch is the only one that can get me my money,' snapped Abramov. 'And if you want to get paid, you're going to have to find her.'

He stomped across the sand, kicked a smoking remnant of timber to one side, then threw back his head and roared at the sky above.

His men stood silently, their bodies alert, watching him.

His shoulders heaving as he tried to get his anger under control, he pointed to the waiting vehicles.

'Find them,' he snarled. 'Hunt them down. Kill the man. Leave the woman for me.'

THIRTY-FIVE

An hour after leaving the Polisario soldiers to hunt down the Russian military enterpriser and his men, Dan cut the engine of the vehicle and ran his hand over his eyes.

They'd reached the UN compound at Mahbes without further incident, and it was all Dan could do to explain their presence to the young soldiers at the gatehouse before wanting to collapse from exhaustion.

An urgent meeting had been organised with the commanding officer, and now Dan led Anna through the rabbit warren of passages that intersected the building, their footsteps echoing off the bare concrete walls as they followed their guide.

The vehicle they'd taken from Salim's men

remained parked at the gatehouse, and Dan had no doubt that it would be appropriated by one of the locals who worked at the UN camp.

When they'd arrived, the two guards who manned the barrier had eyed them warily, suspicious of the two dirty figures who leaned out the windows – until they'd heard the Western accents.

Dan had drummed his fingers impatiently on the steering wheel, checking his mirrors while he explained his and Anna's predicament.

A phone call had been made, an order issued, and the barrier was finally raised to let the vehicle through before dropping back into place, the guards waving them on.

Anna had breathed a sigh of relief.

Dan noticed how utterly weary she looked and resolved to end her ordeal as soon as he could.

The UN soldier who had met them at the main building that served as the headquarters for the region stopped at the end of the passageway and knocked on a door.

A muffled order reached Dan's ears before the door was opened and the soldier announced their arrival, stepping to one side and beckoning to them.

'The major will see you now.'

Dan thanked him and let Anna pass before following her into the room.

The door closed behind him, and as his eyes adjusted to the bright light pooling through the window to his left, he made out a plain room furnished with two filing cabinets, a desk, and a moth-worn chair, next to which a tall man in UN uniform stood and offered his hand.

'Dan Taylor, Anna Collins? I understand you have had quite an ordeal,' he said as they made their introductions. 'Please, sit.' He gestured to two plastic chairs opposite his and lowered his large frame back into his seat, an audible creak escaping from the furniture as he settled his weight onto it.

The UN officer had the same exhausted look as many of Dan's colleagues had had after spending several months at a time in a war zone. His eyes were bloodshot at the corners, and he fidgeted in his seat, unable to relax, his hands shuffling papers across the desk as if he needed to remain busy.

Despite there being no outward conflict in the northern reaches of Western Sahara, no doubt the effort of keeping the peace between the Sahrawis and the occupying Moroccan forces, not to mention the daily threat of militant attacks, was beginning to wear the major down.

Dan understood the man's predicament, but his

own priorities won over any need to exchange pleasantries and extend his sympathy, and he was relieved when the officer got straight to the point.

'How can I help?'

Dan leaned forward. 'First of all, I'd like to use your phone.'

'Certainly. May I ask why? You told my adjutant it was urgent, but nothing more. What's going on?'

Dan sighed. 'All I can say at this point is that I need to make a call to my people back at the office,' he said, keeping up the appearance of being employed by Anna's company. 'We're a day late phoning in, they have no idea if we're okay, and I'm sure if we don't act fast, they'll be making all sorts of calls to embassies in Laâyoune.'

He sat back, waiting for the major's reaction.

The skin under the man's left eye twitched, and he rubbed his chin. 'That would be unfortunate,' he said eventually. His eyes ran over the state of Dan and Anna. 'I expect you need somewhere to stay this evening as well?'

'That would be great, thanks.'

The major nodded. 'There is a guesthouse across the street from the guardhouse. It's where the diplomats stay, journalists and the like, too. I'm sure you'll find it adequate.' He picked up the phone on his desk. 'I'll ask the adjutant to arrange payment.' His mouth quirked. 'I'm presuming your money was stolen?'

'Yes, thanks.'

Dan leaned back in his chair and caught Anna's gaze while the army officer spoke into the phone.

'We'll get a phone call through to David,' he murmured. 'And make sure someone can meet us at the border tomorrow, okay?'

'Yes.'

The major finished his call and stood. 'You can use this phone,' he explained, and pushed it across the table. 'I'll be outside when you're finished.'

'Thanks.'

Dan waited until the door closed behind him, then dialled Mel's number from memory.

The line crackled but connected within two rings, and Dan breathed a sigh of relief.

'It's us. We made it to Mahbes.'

Mel whooped at the end of the line, and Dan held the receiver away from his ear.

'Dan?' David's voice came on the line. 'Are you okay?'

'A little roughed up, but yeah, we're good.' Dan raised an eyebrow at Anna, and she nodded. 'Can you get someone to meet us at the border tomorrow?'

'Sure can. We have someone on standby waiting for our call. He'll be there by oh nine hundred hours and will wait for you.'

'Good.' Dan calculated the distance in his head. 'It'll probably take us three hours to get there.'

'Can you get to a computer to get the information to us?'

'Negative,' said Dan 'We were captured by tribesmen working for the Russians. They took Anna's hard drive—'

'Dammit.'

'Wait. Anna says Benji encrypted the information he uploaded to a cloud drive. She has the codes and can download the information as soon as we get back.'

A long silence greeted his words, and Dan frowned, and then stared at the receiver. 'Hello?'

'I'm here,' said David. 'Listen, Dan? If Anna is the only one who has those codes, you *have* to get her out of there alive. Do you understand?'

Dan turned so Anna couldn't read his expression. 'I know,' he said, keeping his voice even. 'I'm fully aware of that.'

'Watch your back, Taylor. And get to that rendezvous.'

'Copy that.'

Dan replaced the receiver in the cradle and

exhaled. His eyes found the clock on the wall next to the window.

Ten hours remained until it would be light enough to drive.

He rubbed his hands over his face, then stretched his arms over his head.

'What now?' asked Anna.

He smiled. 'I think it's time we checked out the guesthouse,' he said. 'Do you think they serve cold beer?'

As they crossed the room, the door opened, and the major stepped over the threshold.

'Everything okay?'

'Yes, thanks,' said Dan. 'We thought we might go and check into the guesthouse, if that's all right with you?'

'Of course. We've made arrangements for you to stay the night. Perhaps we could have another chat in the morning, when you've had time to rest.'

'Sure,' said Dan.

'It would be good to obtain any information you can about the people who held you captive,' said the major as he led the way back through the building towards the heavily armoured front doors. 'Not to mention how you came to be stranded so far away from the major highways. The more we can pass onto the Polisario, the more we can ensure peace is retained in this region.'

'I understand.'

The major held the door open for them and held out his hand. 'Then I will see you at oh nine hundred hours tomorrow,' he said. A trace of a smile crossed his lips. 'You'll get plenty of rest between now and then.'

'Thanks.'

Dan and Anna made their farewells, then walked through the compound towards the gatehouse.

'We'll leave the vehicle here,' said Dan as they passed it. 'It's probably safer.'

'You didn't tell him the truth. Why?'

'We know the policeman was corrupt,' said Dan. 'Why not everyone else?'

'Oh.'

'Come on,' he said, and took her arm to guide her across the street to the front door of the guesthouse. 'It's beer o'clock.'

THIRTY-SIX

Dan kept his hand on the small of Anna's back as they crossed the threshold to the hotel's bar. They had checked in and decided to have a drink first, grab something to eat, and then freshen up.

Dan's gaze flickered over the room as he passed, noting the lack of security. Evidently no dignitaries or other VIPs were attending the small town.

As drinking holes went, the bar was basic, and as Dan cast his eyes around the space, he realised the room had once been the living area of the original house, converted to its current use as the need arose.

The current clientele resembled a motley crew of easily identifiable aid workers, various government officials, and hangers-on. Dan glared at every single one of them as he guided Anna past the tables, their interest in the young American woman all too apparent.

He steered her towards the bar at the end, resisted the urge to take a running dive at the beer fridge covered in a thin layer of condensation, and instead waited until the lone bar man approached them.

The man's features were tired, resolved to his fate in a small community that bore the brunt of armed conflict, and he raised his eyes to Dan's reluctantly.

Dan glanced at Anna, who nodded.

'Two beers please,' he said. 'From the back of the fridge. The coldest ones you've got.'

The man's shoulders sagged as if he'd been given his last rites before he busied himself with fetching the bottles, muttering under his breath.

Dan turned, leaned an elbow against the bar, and murmured into Anna's ear. 'Friendly place.'

Her mouth twitched. 'They serve beer, and it's the only hotel in town. We can't afford to be fussy.'

'True.'

'You're English?'

Dan turned to his left at the voice to find a man in his thirties on a bar stool, his hands wrapped around a half-full beer bottle and a few days' growth on his face. Dan rubbed his own jaw and figured Mahbes could do with a decent barber shop. It'd probably do a roaring trade.

'Yes,' he said.

The man leaned over and offered his hand. 'Lucas Crawford. Associated Press.'

'Canadian accent?'

The man beamed. 'That's right.'

Dan introduced Anna and then paid for their beers before turning his attention to the reporter. 'You're a long way from home.'

The man arched an eyebrow and raised his beer. 'Don't I know it,' he said, before taking a long swig. He put the bottle back on the bar. 'What about you two? What's your story?'

Dan shot Anna a warning glance before he answered. 'We were working for a charity,' he said, and shrugged. 'Roster finished and they don't need us any longer, so we figured we'd head home.'

Crawford narrowed his eyes at Anna. 'You're American?'

'Yeah,' said Anna, and stuck her hands through her belt loops. 'Thought I'd look for some excitement in my life before settling down.'

The reporter laughed raucously. 'You came to the right place for that,' he said, then shook his head. 'Jesus.'

Dan frowned. 'What makes you say that?'

Crawford leaned closer and lowered his voice. 'Rotten as all hell,' he said in a stage whisper.

'In what way?'

Crawford jerked his head towards a table at the back of the small room. 'Let's move. Less ears.'

He threw a glare at the barman who had sidled closer to them before leading the way towards the table he'd indicated.

Dan made sure he sat with his back to the wall and pulled out a chair for Anna to his left.

Crawford slouched in a chair to Dan's right and rubbed his thumb across the condensation on his beer bottle before taking a swig.

'How much do you know about Mahbes?' he said.

Dan shrugged. 'Nothing really. We were just told to get to the UN airfield so we could get a ride across the border. Why?'

'It's at a crossroads,' Crawford explained. 'You've got the Algerian border in that direction,' he said, pointing behind Anna. 'The Polisario are supposed to be policing this side of the Moroccan berm that splits the country in two, except they're dealing with corruption in half their ranks, and then you've got factions of Al Qaeda stirring things up in the middle.'

'And *then*,' the reporter added, 'a group of six Russians turn up twenty-four hours ago, refuse to stay in the hotel here, and disappear into the desert.'

He paused and raised his eyebrow at Dan. 'You didn't see anyone else on your way here?'

Dan nudged Anna under the table to keep her quiet, shook his head, and picked up his beer.

'No,' he said, and took a long swallow. He put the drink down and frowned. 'What's the angle with Al Qaeda?'

The journalist snorted. 'Their usual trick,' he said. 'Infiltrating the refugee camps, stirring up the teenagers and young men – those kids have known nothing except poverty and dispossession. Yes, they're Sahrawi, but they've never been here. They've grown up in Algerian camps. Al Qaeda would love to stir them up enough to cause a war in Western Sahara to kick out Western-supported Morocco. It'd add to the unrest we've already been seeing in west Africa.'

'Where do the Russians fit into all this?' asked Anna.

'I'm not sure,' said Crawford, and leant back in his seat. 'Although I'm trying to follow an angle that they're supplying weapons to someone in the region here.' He shrugged. 'I just can't find out who yet – or why.'

He stood and pointed at Dan and Anna's drinks. 'Another?'

'No, we're good,' said Dan. 'Thanks.'

Dan waited until the journalist was out of earshot and then turned to Anna.

'Interesting. We know the money stolen from the project ended up in Russia,' he said. 'And we figure that's being used to start an uprising using a mercenary force to influence locals.'

'But if they do that, and start a war, that'll weaken the whole region, and Al Qaeda will take advantage,' said Anna.

'So you'd end up with a messed-up situation like Syria,' said Dan. 'Western-backed Morocco on one side; a rebel force saying it's taking back territory for the Sahrawi, even though we know it's because the Russians will use them to get their own hands on the mineral assets Morocco holds; and Al Qaeda or Daesh grabbing territory for themselves. It'd be a disaster.'

Anna leaned on the table. 'So, what do we do?'

Dan frowned. 'Crawford said the Russians were here yesterday but have disappeared. We know Salim had to wait for instructions from someone and couldn't do anything except hold us captive in the meantime. He'd already taken delivery of some weapons, which were destroyed by us.' He tapped his fingers on the table, then stopped abruptly. 'What if the Russians *aren't* sending any more mercenaries?'

'What do you mean?'

Dan checked Crawford's progress at the bar, but the man was deep in conversation with someone else.

'There's another side to the mercenary business,' said Dan. 'Military enterprisers. They raise the cash for the client, put together the mercenary force, but let the commanding officer run the show. The enterpriser simply makes sure there's enough money to go round.'

'So you're saying that Benji and I stumbled on the military enterpriser, not the mercenary group themselves?' said Anna. 'That makes sense.' She drained the last of her beer, then paused as she put the empty bottle on the table. 'Hang on. Crawford said the Russians arrived twenty-four hours ago and disappeared. If the Russians are the military enterprisers, why are they here?'

'Checking on their investment?' suggested Dan. 'Except when they get to the fort, they're going to find Salim dead, and us gone.'

'How come we didn't see them when we were driving here? The Polisario found us.'

'Probably because we were following a well-known route,' said Dan. 'Remember the tracks we drove on? The Russians would take a diversion to get to the fort rather than a direct route. They'd be trying to avoid the Polisario.'

He sighed and finished his beer. 'Just as well I can get you over the border tomorrow. It figures that money won't be used to arm Salim and his men now, but it won't be long before they raise another willing group of mercenaries to take his place. As Crawford said, there aren't many other career options around here.'

THIRTY-SEVEN

Abramov grimaced as his skull narrowly missed bouncing off the window next to him, threw a poisonous look at his driver, and turned his attention back to the caller on the other end of the line, his grip tightening on his phone.

'Nikolai, I can assure you the funding will be in place soon,' he soothed. 'It's a minor issue with one of our banking partners, that's all.'

As the four-wheel drive vehicle ploughed through a series of hardened sand ruts, he shoved his feet into the foot well and switched his phone to his other hand so he could hold onto the strap that hung above the window.

He closed his eyes as the man at the other end berated him.

'I've never let you down before,' he said, keeping his voice even. 'Have I?'

He resisted the urge to exhale as the arms dealer calmed down and instead pinched the bridge of his nose while he listed his requirements.

'I know,' he said as his order was questioned. 'And you know what it's like dealing with them, too. I'm taking charge now. There'll be no more delegating until this is set in motion,' he added. 'I'll be staying here to oversee the shipment when it arrives, and I'll make sure it's stored properly this time.'

His gaze fell to the door mirror.

The glow from the burning fort had disappeared from view, and so far they'd managed to avoid any contact from the Polisario forces that would surely be hunting for any survivors of the attack.

He knew it was dangerous to return to Mahbes, but it was the only place the Englishman and American woman could have headed towards – if they weren't already lost to the desert.

He couldn't rest until he knew for certain.

The arms dealer began reciting a list of what he could provide, and Abramov concentrated on the delivery details. His lips thinned as he listened, realising that the order wouldn't be complete for another three weeks.

He frowned as the vehicle slowed and jerked his head round to ask the driver what was going on when he realised the man had received a call on his mobile and was speaking in muted tones, the phone tucked between his ear and shoulder as he kept the vehicle on course.

The sound of the arms dealer's voice faded as Abramov saw his driver's face pale. He turned to Abramov, his eyes wide.

He blinked, then handed the phone out. 'You need to take this.'

'Nikolai? I'm going to have to call you back. Yes, I know. I'm sorry. We'll finalise the details once you have the shipment ready to leave.' Abramov ended the call and snatched the other phone from his driver. 'This had better be good.'

'It's Markov.'

Abramov sat up in his seat as his driver floored the accelerator once more, his heart rate increasing so fast a sharp pain stabbed at his ribs.

'What happened?'

'She's safe,' said the voice, before the signal was briefly lost. When it returned, Abramov pressed the phone to his ear hard, his knuckles white as he held onto the armrest set into the vehicle's door. 'She's fine.'

'Why are you phoning Peter?' demanded Abramov. 'Your instructions were to only contact me.'

'We couldn't reach you,' said Markov. 'Your phone has been engaged for the past forty minutes. We felt it better to contact you any way we could, under the circumstances.'

Abramov rubbed at his eyes, and then blinked. 'What circumstances?' he demanded. 'What the hell is going on?'

'We had to move her earlier this afternoon,' said Markov. 'We believe the location of the safe house had been compromised.'

'How?'

'We don't know. But our cameras picked up a man and a woman twice within the past thirty-six hours. They're not local. Too well-dressed, even though they were trying to blend in.'

'Are you sure?'

'Positive. They were observing the house from a distance yesterday, a complete circuit. I sent one of the men to follow them, but he lost them at a transit stop. He would've been too exposed if he'd tried to keep up. They were back this afternoon. Probably trying to establish a pattern.'

'Privateers?'

'No. Definitely official.'

'And you weren't followed to your new location?'

Abramov swore. He knew better than to ask where his daughter had been taken. Both he and Markov knew their enemies could be listening in.

'We were extremely careful, given the new threat. I've posted extra lookouts, and the cameras are being monitored twenty-four seven.'

'You've done well; thank you.'

'I'd get her to speak to you, but she's sleeping now.'

Abramov swallowed and cleared his throat. 'Keep me informed of any more breaches to security,' he said brusquely.

'Yes sir.'

Abramov ended the call and handed the phone back to his driver, who tucked it into his jeans pocket, his eyes searching the darkened landscape ahead of him. Abramov noticed the man's jaw clench and chose to ignore him. Peter also had kids at home, but he knew nothing of the threats against Abramov's daughter.

The military enterpriser felt it safer that way. If his men knew their children could be used as a threat to ensure the success of the operation, it was likely they'd mutiny.

He had bigger problems to deal with.

He hit the speed dial option on his phone and waited for the man at the other end to answer.

'Nikolai? It's me. I'm going to need that shipment earlier than three weeks.'

THIRTY-EIGHT

Dan climbed the wooden staircase to the upper level of the run-down hotel and used his key to open the door to the room he'd been allocated.

As he shut the door, he checked the internal one that linked his room to Anna's. She'd declined a second drink and had retired to her room an hour after dinner while Dan continued to talk with the Canadian journalist.

Satisfied the door that separated them was shut, and making a mental note to check on Anna every couple of hours in case she developed signs of delayed shock, he kicked his boots off next to the bed, stripped off his t-shirt, and headed for the bathroom.

He peeled off his jeans and ran the shower water until a hint of warmth filled the small cubicle. He stepped in, closed his eyes, and let out a groan of pleasure as the water ran over his head.

After four days walking and driving through the desert, the dust and dirt turned the water sandstone coloured. He didn't care if he had to put dirty clothes on again in the morning. He just wanted to be clean before he slept.

He reached out for the soap, scrubbed at his skin until it hurt, and then did the same for his hair. The only thing he couldn't do was have a shave – there was no complimentary razor.

Conscious of the need to conserve water, he turned off the faucet and grabbed a towel.

His thoughts turned to what would need to be done the next day. The UN commander had probably commandeered the four-wheel drive vehicle after seeing them to the hotel across the street from his office, so new transport would have to be sought if they couldn't get a flight in one of the small aircraft used to ferry supplies to the remote outpost. After that, there was another two hour drive to the border and the contact David was sending to meet them.

Dan ran a hand over his face and realised he

was almost asleep on his feet. The bed had looked inviting, despite his suspicions the mattress had probably worn thin from decades of use.

He wrapped the towel around his waist and opened the door.

He yelped in shock and took a step back.

Anna stood in the middle of his room, her hair wet and her t-shirt knotted around a slim waist. Her jeans clung to her hips, the top button of her fly undone. Her eyes found his, and she trailed her hand from her throat towards her breasts.

'Can I stay here tonight?' she said.

Dan swallowed and then held up a finger. 'Give me a minute. Stay there. Don't move.'

He closed the bathroom door, ran a hand through his damp hair, and swore under his breath.

'Get a grip,' he muttered.

He reached out and turned the cold tap in the sink on full, then ran his hands under the water and splashed his face, his mind racing.

He was in a foreign land, had recently survived kidnapping and likely death, and now a beautiful twenty-something half-naked blonde woman was standing in the middle of his hotel room, offering herself for sex.

The same woman whose father happened to be

a good friend, and who had a private army he'd have no hesitation sending after Dan if he found out he'd bedded his daughter.

Dan turned the water off and cast his eyes around the small room until he located the pair of jeans he'd discarded on the floor before stepping into the shower.

He unwrapped the towel from his waist, threw it over the rail next to the sink, and tugged the jeans on. He caught sight of himself in the mirror, bare chest exposing a criss-cross pattern of scars. His face, neck, and arms had borne the brunt of the prolonged exposure to the sun over the past four days and were already turning browner than he'd seen since his time in the Middle East.

He half-shrugged and supposed some women would find him attractive.

If they had recently survived kidnapping and likely death.

Despite a lack of a regimented workout for the past year, he'd kept fit by running circuits of the marina in Essaouria every morning since his arrival. It served both as an exercise regime and as a way to monitor any suspicious activity.

He snorted under his breath as he recalled the yacht explosion, then sighed as he straightened, turned away from the mirror, and twisted the door handle.

Anna stood in the middle of his room, arms hugging her body, her face a picture of misery. When she saw him, she dropped her hands to her side.

'I'm sorry. I should never have done that.' She looked up at the stained ceiling, blinked hard, and then exhaled. 'I should go.'

'Hey,' he said, crossing the space between them in two strides, 'you've been through a traumatic experience. It's only natural to seek comfort in another human being.' He squeezed her arm, moved past her, and grabbed the t-shirt he'd tossed onto the bed. He pulled it over his head and faced her once more. 'But we're not having sex. Your father would kill me for a start.'

He moved back to her as she sniffed loudly and reached out to push a strand of hair behind her ear. 'And I care about you too much.'

Anna nodded, unable to meet his eyes.

'You can stay here tonight, though, if you'd like?' He raised an eyebrow and tilted her chin until their eyes met. 'Nothing's going to happen, but if it'll make you feel safer, then stay.'

A tear rolled down Anna's cheek, and Dan brushed it away with his thumb.

She exhaled once more, steadied herself, and wiped at her eyes. 'Thank you.'

Dan smiled. 'I don't know about you, but I need to sleep. I'm shattered.'

He moved to the bed, pulled the sheets aside, and propped a pillow against the headboard before beckoning to Anna. 'Come on.'

Anna choked out a laugh but kicked off her shoes and padded across the floor, sliding across the mattress to where Dan lay.

He waited until she'd settled into the crook of his arm.

'We'll leave at first light,' he said. 'That'll give us time to rest for a few hours. We'll take all the water we can from the vending machine downstairs, too.'

'Do you think we'll be able to get our vehicle back before the major finds us?'

'I can't imagine he'll be in his office until six o'clock at least,' said Dan. 'And he's not expecting us until nine.'

Anna managed a low chuckle. 'You think we'd be spoiling his lie-in otherwise?'

'Something like that. No, we'll just have to see if we can charm our way past the guards at the gatehouse. I'm sure they won't be keen to wake their boss up just so we can take our vehicle to refuel it before setting off, do you?'

'Sounds perfectly reasonable to me.'

Dan wrapped an arm around Anna's shoulder and pulled her to him, stroking her hair.

'Sleep,' he murmured. 'I won't let anyone hurt you.'

THIRTY-NINE

Dan blinked in the darkness and raised his head off the pillow, all his senses alert.

There was a moment's silence, and then a scream and the sound of suppressed gunfire filled the air.

Dan rolled off the bed pulling Anna with him. She woke as they hit the floor.

'Dan? What the hell?'

'Shh. The hotel's under attack.'

'Wha—'

'Where are your shoes? Put them on. We're leaving.'

Dan squinted at the ancient radio alarm clock on the table next to the bed.

Three o'clock in the morning.

The perfect time for an ambush.

Dan crawled across the floor to where he'd discarded his boots, sat down, and pulled them on, then inched across to the window and carefully raised his head above the sill.

The guardhouse on the opposite side of the street appeared deserted, the compound beyond floodlit under a swathe of powerful lights that cast the rest of the road into shadows.

Movement beneath his position caught his eye, and he moved back.

Two men in black fatigues were in the road outside, guarding the front entrance to the building, their hands wrapped around assault rifles.

Dan noticed the way they held the weapons and quickly concluded the men were professionals, unlike Salim's rag-tag group of followers.

He heard movement in the street below the window and lowered his head as both men turned, their heads snapping round in unison as a figure lurched out of the shadows and began to run from the hotel, towards the UN compound.

'Shit,' he murmured, as he realised it was Crawford, trying to escape. 'Idiot. Why didn't you just try to hide?'

He grimaced as both armed men brought their rifles up at the same time and fired.

The journalist didn't stand a chance.

'Dan?'

He moved back to Anna, who crouched next to the bed, her eyes wide.

'It's the Russians, isn't it?'

'I think so, yes.'

'What are we going to do?'

'Follow me.'

He grabbed her hand and hurried to the door that separated their rooms. Checking the space was clear and the door to the hallway was closed, he hurried to the window and dropped to his knees, pulling Anna down with him.

The window to her room faced the back of the hotel, and if Crawford's information had been correct, then the Russian team comprised six men – two of whom were out front guarding the street.

'Won't the guards at the UN compound help?' asked Anna.

Dan shook his head. 'I don't think the guards are going anywhere,' he said. 'The guardhouse was deserted – I didn't see anyone appear when Crawford started running towards it. I'm guessing whoever was on duty has been killed. It could be a while before anyone discovers them. We're sure as hell not hanging around to find out.'

He motioned to her to stay down, then moved

forward and ran his fingers under the window sash. He closed his eyes, hoped the fitting had been oiled recently, and pulled.

The window slid open easily, and he breathed a sigh of relief as he crouched once more and got his bearings.

Shouting from the floor below reached them, and Anna moved closer. He reached out and squeezed her hand while his mind raced.

There would be at least two men clearing the rooms one by one, a methodical process that would ensure they didn't miss their intended targets. That meant at least one, maybe two men, patrolling the lower level in case anyone tried to escape.

Which left no-one to patrol the back of the building.

He hoped.

He raised himself on his haunches until he could peer over the window ledge to the ground below.

A sheer drop of several metres yawned before him.

He glanced over his shoulder to the unmade bed, an idea forming.

'Ever read the *Famous Five* when you were a kid?' he asked.

'Who?'

'Never mind.'

Dan crawled across the floor, pulled the sheets from the bed and knotted the two lengths together. He tied one end to the leg of a solid wooden dresser that bore the pock-marked scars of cigarette burns across its surface, and then stuck his head out the window once more.

'All right,' he said, turning to Anna, 'you're out first. When you get to the ground, stay low. I'll be right behind you.'

He wrapped a length of the material around his forearm, then guided Anna over the sill and held her by the arm until she had a firm grip on the sheet.

Before she began her descent, he leaned over her shoulder, checked the route was still clear, and then nodded.

'Go.'

She dropped from sight quickly, hand over fist, using her feet to walk down the outer wall. Within seconds, Dan felt the sheet go slack and peered out.

Anna was already scuttling towards the shell of an abandoned car in the shadows.

Dan pulled the sheet to test the knot around the leg of the dresser, then eased himself through the window opening and began his own climb.

He had passed the empty bedroom below Anna's when he heard a shout.

Above his head, the door to Anna's bedroom crashed open, a single shot ringing out as the first man burst across the threshold, and Dan realised he was out of time.

He peered down, gauging the drop.

It was only a few metres, but he could still risk breaking an ankle.

'There'd better be bloody lashings of ginger beer after this,' he muttered through clenched teeth.

He swore under his breath, and let go.

FORTY

Dan hit the ground with a grunt and rolled, taking the impact away from his body.

He didn't wait to see if the attackers had spotted him; he crouched over and ran to where Anna waited, took her by the arm, and pulled her away from the hotel.

'Move!'

A shout rang out from behind them, and he urged another spurt of energy from his body as gunfire rang out in the street.

Dan pulled Anna into an alleyway two blocks away from the guesthouse and slipped behind a pile of stinking refuse that had been dumped next to a well-secured door. He motioned to Anna to join him and then froze as something ran across his foot.

He gritted his teeth, not wanting to alarm the woman next to him, and kicked out at the furry creature, a loud squeak confirming his aim was true.

'Was that a rat?' hissed Anna.

'Large mouse,' murmured Dan. He motioned to her to hunker down behind the debris and tried not to think how many more of the rodents were in the near vicinity.

He had bigger issues to worry about.

He peered round the corner of the building and checked the progress of the armed Russians; after they'd fired shots in Dan's wake, the two men clearing the guesthouse rooms had returned to the ground floor and were now standing in front of the building, arguing with a taller man who appeared to be their leader.

Dan's eyes narrowed, and he cursed under his breath as the man turned away, his face falling into shadow before Dan had managed to get a clear view of his features.

He gave himself a mental shake. First priority had to be getting Anna away from danger. Once that was done, he'd allow himself to track down the Russian leader, but not before.

He jerked his head back as a bright light illuminated the street beyond the alleyway from the direction they'd just run from, closely followed by engines roaring.

'What's going on?' whispered Anna.

'I think the major found out the gatehouse has been compromised,' said Dan. 'Come on – this could work in our favour.'

He realised their chances were perilously few, but if the UN troops were going to exit the compound and approach the guesthouse with force, he wanted to take advantage of the situation.

He grabbed Anna's hand and led the way back along the wall towards the street, then peered round the corner.

Sure enough, the UN compound was ablaze with floodlights that hung from gantries, illuminating the two large trucks that were being readied.

Dan inched forwards a little further, trying to see where the Russians were.

A dark form flashed past the entrance to the guesthouse, closely followed by another, and then the sound of engines being started at the back of the property reached his ears.

'Shit, they're going to get away.'

'Won't the UN troops chase them?' said Anna.

'They're probably not allowed to,' replied Dan. 'I'd be very surprised if they did.'

They hung back as one by one, three black four-wheel drive vehicles sped past them, heading west out of the small community.

As the dust settled on the road, the UN troops emerged from their vehicle, fanned out, and began taking control of the situation at the guesthouse.

Patrons gradually emerged from the building, visibly shaken by the assault, while soldiers performed triage duties and shouted into radios over the noise of the crowd that had gathered in the aftermath.

'Let's go,' said Dan.

He led Anna away from the alley entrance, waited until a second UN vehicle passed, then crossed the street in its wake and pulled her into the shadows with him.

'Not a word,' he murmured.

Anna nodded in response.

He waited until the replacement guardsmen's attention was taken by a third vehicle exiting the compound and then slipped past and led Anna towards a row of UN vehicles parked beside the four-wheel drive they'd taken from Salim.

There was no point in trying to escape in the same vehicle they'd arrived in – the Russians would be instantly alerted to their presence.

Instead, Dan hurried past each of the UN

vehicles until he found one that met his requirements.

The door was unlocked.

'At the rate I'm going this week,' Dan muttered, 'I could always have a new career as a professional car thief.'

'Why this vehicle?' Anna demanded. 'Why not take something a little less conspicuous?'

'Are you kidding me? Next time you watch the news, check out the vehicles Al Qaeda and the like are driving around in – they're always stealing old UN vehicles. No-one will take any notice of us, trust me.'

Dan inched the door open and followed Anna through the narrow gap.

Anna crawled over the handbrake and settled in the foot well of the passenger seat, her eyes wide as Dan hunched over the steering console and smacked the ignition cover with the heel of his hand.

After the third time, the casing fell away, exposing the wiring, and Dan squinted in the poor light until he located the ones he needed.

The sound of his heartbeat thudded against his eardrums, making it harder to gauge what was happening outside the vehicle. He raised his head above the dashboard and peered through the windscreen.

The major was nowhere in sight, and the only men left at the gate looked young and inexperienced, their faces reflecting the horror of the cold-blooded execution of their colleagues.

Dan's eyes found Anna's. 'We don't stop once we start,' he said, 'so brace yourself. Things could get messy if they try to stop us.'

She nodded and reached out, seeking handholds to wedge herself firmly in place.

Dan pinched the wires together; the starter motor coughed once, and then he hit the accelerator, releasing the handbrake at the same time.

Dan switched up through the gears in rapid succession, the young guardsmen's eyes opening wide as they turned to see what was going on within their own compound. The men jumped to one side as Dan roared past.

He spun the wheel hard left, the back of the four-wheel drive sliding over the uneven surface of the road outside the compound, and then accelerated past the guesthouse.

'They're not shooting at us,' said Anna, peering over the sill of the window next to her. She glanced over her shoulder at him. 'Won't they try to stop us?'

'Not with force,' said Dan. 'Like I said, most UN compounds like this one have orders to maintain a watching brief, nothing else.' His mouth quirked. 'Plus they might feel a bit awkward about shooting at one of their own vehicles.'

As Dan flung the wheel to the right, taking them further away from the guesthouse, Anna climbed out of the foot well and fastened her seatbelt.

'Shouldn't we have asked the major to help us?'

Dan shook his head. 'I've got a funny feeling about the major,' he admitted. 'Okay, the Russians would have worked out for themselves that we'd head to Mahbes – it's the only community around for miles, let's face it – but that fast? And who told them we were at the guesthouse? For all they knew, we could've been in the compound.'

'You think the major told the Russians where we were?' Anna's tone was incredulous.

'Or one of his men did,' said Dan. 'Or someone at the guesthouse. Maybe.' He shrugged. 'I figure we're better off putting as much distance as possible between ourselves and Mahbes.'

As the last buildings fell away at the side of the road, Dan increased his speed.

'So, now what do we do?'

'Aim for the border and our meeting point,' said Dan. 'And hopefully our contact is on time.'

The sun was cresting the horizon as Dan steered the UN vehicle up onto the asphalt and joined the main road that bisected the Moroccan-Western Saharan border.

A faded green sign pointed the way, although Dan could already see the towers and wire fencing that divided the two territories. A small crowd gathered at the Western Saharan side in front of him as he pulled the vehicle over and opened the door.

'Come on,' he said. 'We'll walk the rest of the way. The major can send someone to come and get his truck.'

The asphalt was already starting to bake as they climbed from the vehicle and began to walk towards the border post, and despite their having freshened up at the guesthouse the previous evening, Dan knew they looked bedraggled.

He trusted that David's contact would bring passports for Anna and himself, as well as any other documentation to ease their passage from the territory.

He glanced over his shoulder, the hair on the back of his neck prickling.

'What's wrong?'

He turned at the note of panic in Anna's voice and forced a smile. 'Nothing. Being paranoid, that's all.'

They fell into a companionable silence as they joined the back of the pedestrian queue. A weather-beaten truck belching diesel fumes rumbled to a standstill next to them, and despite the stink from the exhaust, Dan was grateful for the shade the vehicle provided.

He waited until Anna turned to face the front of the queue and then checked the road behind them once more.

He unclenched his fists and forced himself to relax. He moved his head from side to side, a satisfying *crack* emanating from his neck muscles, and moved closer to Anna as the line of people shuffled forward.

He stared at his feet, rehearsing his words to the border guards, when a low whistle reached him from the front of the queue.

He raised his eyes and grinned.

A familiar figure leaned against the border post, his arms folded across his chest and a relieved expression on his face.

'About time,' said Mitch Frazer, and checked his watch. 'What the bloody hell took you so long?'

FORTY-ONE

Dan opened the back door of the four-wheel drive, waited until Anna had climbed inside, and then took the passenger seat, allowing his colleague to take the wheel.

After everything that had happened, relief flooded his tired body that he and Anna were in capable hands, although he wouldn't let his guard down completely until they were far away from the border crossing.

Mitch accelerated away as Dan closed the door, leaving a cloud of dust in their wake.

'We got word of the attack at the UN compound and the hotel a few hours ago,' Mitch explained as he guided the vehicle around a pothole in the worn asphalt. 'Figured it'd be something to do with you two.'

'Russians,' said Dan. 'Although whether the person funding this whole attempted coup was amongst them, I don't know – I'm presuming he was. I didn't hang around to ask.'

He shuffled in his seat until he could see the road behind in the wing mirror, the border post receding in the distance.

'Do you think they'll follow us?'

Anna's voice carried from the back seat, and Dan caught Mitch's eye as he twisted round to speak to her.

He swallowed and then figured it'd be best to tell her the truth.

'Yes. I do,' he said. He reached out and squeezed her hand. 'Don't you?'

She nodded, her eyes downcast. 'It's too important to them, isn't it?' She sighed. 'I mean, they didn't put all this effort into their planning and the theft to simply walk away, did they?'

'No.'

'How do you want to do this?' said Mitch. He jerked his chin at the narrow road in front of them, the traffic already beginning to thin out as merchants returned to their communities along the route. 'Another half an hour, this road is going to be empty, and we'll be on our own. Nothing but sand dunes for company.'

Dan mulled it over for a moment. 'The only thing that will work is to lead them to us on purpose, but make sure we have the advantage somehow.'

'I might be able to help there,' said Mitch.

'How?'

'Wait and see.'

Forty minutes later, they'd reached the dunes.

Mitch pulled the vehicle over to the side of the road, drove towards the base of the dunes, and put the four-wheel drive into neutral.

'They'll be here soon. Come on,' he said, opening his door. 'I've got something to show you.'

He led the way round to the back of the vehicle, wrenched open the door, threw the water canisters onto the back seat, and then tugged the carpet underneath away.

Dan's eyes opened wide at the sight before him. 'You came prepared.'

An array of weaponry glistened under the sun's glare, including assault rifles, 9mm pistols, and plenty of ammunition.

'What do you fancy?' said Mitch, unable to suppress the grin on his face.

Dan pointed at the one of the assault rifles.

'That for a start,' he said, then pushed a blanket aside, revealing the dull sheen of a rifle favoured by snipers. He raised an eyebrow at Mitch. 'How the hell did you get your hands on that out here?'

Mitch winked. 'Contacts,' he said, and handed the weapon to Dan. 'Okay, you take that – I'll provide cover fire,' he added, picking up another rifle.

He turned to the others. 'Six of them, three of us,' he said, his eyes finding Anna's. 'Reckon you can do it?'

Anna nodded. 'Yes.' She suddenly looked weary. 'If we don't stop them, they're never going to stop until they kill us, will they?'

'No,' said Dan. 'They won't.' He turned and surveyed the empty landscape. 'There's no-one around for miles to help us.'

Mitch pointed to a low rise. 'We can position ourselves there. Leave the vehicle behind the dune to act as a bit of protection. Anna can cover our rear flank while you and I pick them off as they approach.'

Dan squinted in the bright light as he mulled over Mitch's plan, then nodded. 'Let's do it.'

FORTY-TWO

Dan slammed the door shut, and they climbed back in the vehicle, Mitch expertly steering it through the dunes before doubling back and braking to a halt behind their intended position.

They piled out, and Dan waited while Mitch selected a rifle and pistol for Anna before he slammed the door shut and locked it, handing the keys to Anna.

She took them from him, a frown creasing her brow.

'In case something goes wrong,' explained Dan. 'We need to know you can get away from here without us.'

She swallowed, pocketed the keys, and chambered a round in her gun before making sure the safety was on. She tucked it into her waistband, and then readied the rifle. She cleared her throat and eyed them both. 'Better make sure nothing goes wrong then, right?'

Mitch laughed and began to climb the dune.

Dan closed the gap between himself and Anna and pulled her into a hug.

'Keep your head down and your eyes open. They *will* try to outflank us.'

'I know,' she mumbled into his chest. She stepped away and looked up at him. 'Go on – go. They'll be here soon.'

Dan turned on his heel and followed the tracks of Mitch's footsteps up the dune, the soft sand sinking under his weight as he climbed, making progress slow.

Mitch had already taken a position on the crest of the dune by the time he reached him, his body splayed out above Dan, his rifle aimed at the direction from which they'd travelled. He glanced up as Dan dropped beside him.

'You realise if word gets out about this, we could be responsible for an international incident?'

The corner of Dan's mouth twitched. 'Best keep it quiet then.'

Mitch shook his head. 'Here they come,' he

muttered, and jerked his chin towards the vehicle below them. 'Do you think she'll be okay?'

'She can shoot, that's for sure,' said Dan. 'Even if she manages to hold them off enough for us to halve their numbers on this side, it's going to help.'

'What if we can't?'

'Glass half full, Mitch,' Dan murmured as he settled his eye against the rifle scope. 'Glass half full.'

He heard Mitch exhale and willed his heartbeat to calm.

Through the lens of the scope, he could make out three black vehicles hurtling across the valley between the dunes, a cloud of dusty sand in their wake. Sunlight glinted off the windscreens as they turned into the line of dunes that concealed Dan and Mitch's position, the vehicles' rugged long-travel suspension allowing them to bounce easily over the small rocks that had thrown Mitch's own vehicle around so badly.

Dan swallowed, adrenalin beginning to flow through his veins. He fought down the sensation and tried to focus on his breathing instead.

Silence stretched between the two men as each of them concentrated on their targets.

'I've got clear line of sight on the driver of the first vehicle,' said Mitch.

'Take the shot.'

Dan kept his eye pressed to the rifle scope as the report from Mitch's weapon assaulted his hearing.

A split second later, the windscreen of the first vehicle imploded, and the four-wheel drive swerved sharply to its left, careening out of control until it landed nose-first in a dune, facing away from Dan and Mitch's position.

As a second man stumbled out the passenger door, Mitch fired again, and then cursed.

'Missed him. He's gone to ground.'

Dan didn't answer. He was too busy concentrating on the second and third vehicles that were taking evasive manoeuvres, zig-zagging their way closer to the dune where he lay.

Although Mitch's shot had disabled one of the vehicles and killed one of their enemy, it had also alerted the rest of the Russians to their position.

Dan fought down the urge to panic, his finger covering the trigger, and held his breath.

He squeezed, the round exiting the rifle at subsonic speed, and the second vehicle ground to a halt as the shot blasted through the windscreen.

The third vehicle slid to a standstill behind the second vehicle, the occupants using it to provide cover as they opened the doors.

Mitch let loose a short burst from his rifle,

sending the driver and passenger scurrying from their vehicle towards the back doors of the third.

Dan heard his teammate emit a grunt of satisfaction as the passenger stumbled, then fell, clutching his leg.

'I'm out.'

Dan aimed at the chest of the fallen man as Mitch ejected the spent magazine from his rifle and reloaded. He hated to kill a man already injured, but he knew if he didn't, Anna would surely die.

He took the shot, a plume of red lifting into the air through his scope as the bullet found its target.

He lifted his gaze to see the driver diving head-first into the back of the third vehicle, and then it was barrelling towards their position once more.

'I still can't see the guy from the first vehicle anywhere,' said Mitch through gritted teeth.

'Anna?' Dan yelled over his shoulder. 'There's one unaccounted for. Keep your eyes open.'

Anna's shouted response carried up the dune.

Dan ignored her and shifted the rifle's position against his body. The last vehicle was close now, and he wanted to be able to manoeuvre quickly if he needed to.

The driver of the vehicle slewed it to a halt at an angle several metres from the dune, and Dan realised they were planning to use it as a barricade.

Sure enough, the doors on the far side opened, and the three occupants dropped to the ground.

'What do you think?' said Mitch.

Dan exhaled. 'One at the front, trying to use the engine block as cover. The other two will be more exposed. One at the rear end, one just behind the guy at the front, but still with less protection.'

'Yeah, agree. Wonder what firepower they have?'

The two men ducked as the Russian at the front of the four-wheel drive vehicle rose up, brought an assault rifle up to his chest, and fired.

'And the answer to that would be – plenty,' Mitch said.

'Use short bursts to keep them down,' said Dan. 'I'll see if I can pick them off. I'll start with the two near the back, okay?'

'Copy that.'

They waited until the man stopped firing, expecting one of the other Russians to begin, but apart from single shots that fell short of their position, none did.

'They must only have handguns,' said Dan. 'Go!'

Mitch raised his head and began firing, short bursts that kicked up the sand around the front of the vehicle below their position, to make sure the Russian with the assault rifle stayed down.

Dan waited a second, then steadied his breathing once more and aimed at the driver's side door. He fired twice, knowing both shots from the large calibre weapon would pierce easily through the soft metal and upholstery of the four-wheel drive.

The second round found its target, a cry echoing across the sand to where Dan lay, before the silhouette of a man's body appeared below the vehicle.

'Halfway there,' murmured Mitch.

Dan ignored him and lined up his next target.

He cursed under his breath as a round scuffed up the sand next to him and forced himself to concentrate. If their pursuers were finding their range, he and Mitch were running out of time.

'Fuck.'

Dan exhaled as Mitch's voice carried across the dune towards him. His finger caressed the trigger, and rounds exploded from the rifle towards the rear of the Russians' vehicle.

At the same time, Mitch fired at the front of the vehicle, keeping the other Russian pinned down where he could do no harm.

The staccato bursts from the Russian's assault

rifle fell silent an instant before the shooter's prone form collapsed within sight, his arms flailing in the sand at the front of the vehicle before he stilled.

A moment later, Dan's aim found its mark, a muted shout emanating from the rear of the vehicle, and the gunfire fell silent.

Dan closed his eyes, removed his finger from the trigger, and wiped the sweat from his brow.

'Good work,' murmured Mitch.

They both spun round at the sound of Anna's scream.

Below them, the Russian who had escaped the first vehicle snaked his arm around Anna's neck and pressed the barrel of his gun to her temple.

His voice carried up the dune with ease. 'Where the *fuck* is my money?'

FORTY-THREE

'Cover me.'

'He'll shoot her.'

'Not if I'm unarmed. I might be able to charm him out of it.'

Mitch swore under his breath. 'I can't get a clear line of sight. You've got to get her to move away from him.'

'Copy that.'

Dan dropped his rifle, threw his handgun to one side, and slid down the dune away from Mitch towards the Russian and Anna, slowing his descent as best he could to avoid alarming her assailant further.

He stopped several metres away, dug his boots into the sand to steady himself, and held up his hands, a plume of dust cascading down the dune to where Anna and her captive stood.

'Let her go.'

In response, the Russian snaked his arm tighter around Anna's neck.

She whimpered and tried to move her head away, but she was held firm.

Dan avoided the urge to check over his shoulder and see what angle Mitch had on the Russian. By using Anna as a shield, the man was effectively blocking any shot Mitch could possibly take.

The Russian nudged the radio clipped to his collar.

'Mikhail? Mikhail?'

A hiss of static burst from the device.

'Mikhail is dead, pal,' said Mitch, his voice carrying down the dune. 'Along with the rest of your team.'

'You lie!' the Russian spat.

Dan raised an eyebrow. 'You think we'd be having such a convivial chat if your friends were still firing at us?' He jerked his thumb over his shoulder. 'They'd be here by now, wouldn't they?'

He frowned as he felt movement beneath his feet, closely followed by a faint *boom*.

'Drop your weapon!' yelled Mitch.

A sly smile crossed the Russian's face, and he pressed the barrel of the gun tighter to Anna's head.

Dan tried to focus. Something wasn't right; an almost musical tone filled the air for a split second and then faded.

A frown creased the Russian's brow, and his grip relaxed on Anna's arm.

Anna didn't waste time. She drove her heel into the man's instep, and he fell away, crying out in pain.

A single *crack* passed the air next to Dan, and the next moment, the Russian dropped his gun as his hand flew to his arm, blood pouring from the bullet wound.

The Russian's eyes opened wide as he lifted his chin. His gaze travelled beyond Dan to where Mitch was standing, and his mouth fell open.

Dan could see the fear in the man's face as his mouth worked soundlessly. He kept his eyes on the Russian, but his mind was racing, even as the man raised his hand and pointed beyond Mitch's position.

Again, a *boom* reverberated off the dune, and for a fleeting moment he wondered if the Moroccan air force had scrambled jets nearby and the sonic rush of air was causing the noise.

Then his geologist mind caught up, and his

heart lurched at the same time the sand beneath his feet began to slide. He spun round.

'Avalanche!' he yelled as he saw the dune begin to collapse behind his teammate. 'Mitch – get down from there!'

He turned back to Anna. 'Go!'

He pointed beyond the parked four-wheel drive.

Anna nodded and took off.

Dan pivoted as Mitch tumbled into him, and the pair of them slid to the bottom of the dune, the sound of rushing sand at their heels.

They overtook the Russian who was limping away as fast as he could, and as they caught up with Anna, Mitch reached out and grabbed her arm, pulling her along with them.

They slid to a standstill several metres away and turned as one towards the dune.

The collapse had already reached their vehicle, the weight of the sand tipping it at an unnatural angle, and showed no sign of slowing down.

Beyond the vehicle, the Russian was stumbling, his hand covering the bullet wound to his arm. His escape was hindered by the ankle injury Anna had caused and the fact that he kept looking over his shoulder to check the avalanche's progress. As he lurched forward once more, he tripped. He cried out, and his eyes found Dan's.

'Shit.'

'Wait – where are you going?' Mitch yelled.

'He's not going to make it,' Dan called over his shoulder.

'He's not worth it!'

Dan ignored him, pumped his arms and raced back across the sand to where the Russian had now stumbled, the man crawling as fast as he could. Despite everything, he couldn't leave another man to die like this, not after all the lives he'd already taken to keep Anna safe.

The fall of the avalanche had already reached the Russian's feet and was quickly coating his legs in a fine dust, piling up around him. He desperately clawed at the encroaching sand, trying to pull himself free from the weight that was rapidly burying him alive.

Dan dropped to his knees. 'Give me your hand.'

The Russian continued to sweep at the sand, and Dan realised if they didn't move fast, he too would be buried.

He reached out, grabbed the man under his arms, and pulled.

The Russian swore and tried to kick his legs

free, but the weight of the sand was too much. He looked up, and Dan saw the panic in his eyes.

Dan pulled again, sweat pouring down his brow with the effort, ignoring the dust that was already covering his feet and swelling against his ankles, but the Russian's legs remained trapped.

Behind, he could hear Mitch and Anna yelling, and he raised his gaze to the dune they'd run from.

The four-wheel drive was now buried, lost from view, and a second avalanche wave was tearing down the slope towards him.

'Shit.'

'Go.'

Dan glanced down.

The Russian was staring at him, his jaw clenched, his eyes resolute.

Dan growled under his breath and lifted his chin to check the avalanche's progress.

It was too damn close.

His attention jerked back to the Russian as a hand snaked around his calf muscle, and Dan's eyebrows shot up as he saw the man was holding out a photograph to him, desperation in his eyes.

'My daughter,' he gasped. 'Kozlow will kill her now. You have to stop him. Please, tell her I loved her.'

Dan prised the photograph from the man's fingers.

In it, the Russian stood with his arms around the shoulders of a gangly teenager, both of them wrapped up warm in ski clothing, smiling for the camera.

He tore his eyes away at the Russian's next words.

'Go!'

Dan swallowed and nodded.

He took one last look at the rising cloud of sand, made sure the photograph was tucked safely into his pocket, and then turned and ran.

The bellow of the collapsing dune reached his ears as he forced himself to run faster, Mitch and Anna beckoning him to hurry, their voices lost in the cacophony that surrounded him.

In his mind, he could feel the avalanche licking at his heels, eager to claim him as it surely had the Russian by now. Dan fought down the terror and cursed under his breath.

Mitch and Anna remained where they were, only fifty or so metres away, and Dan checked over his shoulder before slowing to a stop.

He leaned forward and rested his hands on his knees, his eyes flickering over the ground before him sightlessly.

The blue sky had been obliterated, the air around him peppered with the sand that had been lifted with such incredible force from its original location.

Now, an ominous silence blanketed the area. The rumbling from the dunes had ceased, the only sign that anything had happened being a slight settling of the sand around Dan's feet.

Grit filled his mouth, and he spat to one side and straightened.

Mitch joined him, his arms crossed over his rifle. 'We'd better check for signs of life, to be sure.'

Dan nodded. 'We have to wait a few minutes. In case there's another collapse.'

'Have you ever seen anything like that before?'

Dan shook his head. 'Only under controlled conditions.' A shiver ran down his spine. 'What a way to bloody go.'

Anna joined them, her breathing ragged.

Dan instinctively placed his arm around her shoulders, and the three of them stood for a moment, staring at the cloud of ochre-coloured dust as it slowly settled to the ground.

'All right,' said Dan. He sighed. 'We'll check on the Russian, then salvage what we can from the vehicle. We'll take the Russians' four-wheel drive from the front of the dune – if it hasn't been buried as well.'

They walked forward, three abreast, all of them wary of stumbling over the Russian's body.

Several metres from where they started, Dan found him: a dusty mound rising up from the new plain that had been carved out by the passing sand. The force of the avalanche had pushed the man's body a long way from where Dan had tried to rescue him.

Now, he crouched and gently rolled the man over, sand falling from the man's mouth and nostrils. Dan reached out and placed his fingers against the man's neck, even though he knew it was pointless.

The man had been buried alive, his lungs full of sand, his petrified eyes wide and staring.

Dan fought down the urge to gag and closed the man's eyes before standing and brushing his hands on his jeans.

Mitch circled the man's prone form before lowering his weapon and turning to Dan. 'So much for using your wit and charm.'

Anna reached out for Dan.

He gave her hand a reassuring squeeze.

'Is he dead?'

'Yes,' said Dan. 'Now we just need to—'

Anna held up her finger to silence him, then turned and jogged a few paces away before being violently sick.

'Amazing, the effect you have on the ladies,' murmured Mitch.

'Piss off.'

FORTY-FOUR

Dan pulled the last container of water from the back of the third vehicle abandoned by the now-dead Russians and carried it across to the four-wheel drive they intended to use.

They'd wandered amongst the three damaged vehicles, Anna searching for any evidence she could use to prove her case against the Russian military enterpriser once she was back in Rotterdam, while Dan and Mitch sourced water and fuel for their onward journey.

Mitch had used his smartphone to take photographs of the faces of each of the Russian mercenaries, so Mel would be able to pass on the details to the various secret service departments and their contacts. Six less armed assassins on the streets of Europe would be welcome news in some quarters of the establishment.

Dan had briefly debated returning to Essaouria but had quickly discarded the thought, given they had no idea who else might be lying in wait for them, and the fact he still hadn't found out who had destroyed his boat.

Instead, he and Mitch had agreed upon a dash to the northern border with Ceuta, a Spanish-owned territory on the tip of the northern African continent. From there, they could catch an international flight out of the continent, and Anna could return to her home in the United States to be reunited with her family.

'Ready?' asked Mitch, surveying the supplies they'd stacked inside the vehicle.

'That'll do. We probably won't need all of this, but at least it stops anyone else getting their hands on it.'

'True.'

Dan stood back as Mitch swung the back door closed, then opened the rear passenger door for Anna and climbed in next to her while Mitch slid behind the wheel and gunned the engine.

As the vehicle began to bounce over the dunes towards their destination, Dan's eyes wandered over Anna's face and neck.

Splatter from where Mitch had shot the now-dead Russian in the arm covered her pale skin, and she hadn't said a word.

'Come here,' he said.

She slid across the seat to him, and he reached over his shoulder for one of the liberated bottles of water before pulling his t-shirt over his head. He bunched it up and poured some water onto it, soaking the material through, and reached out to Anna.

'That bad, huh?' she murmured.

'Yeah. Can't have you making us look bad when we turn up at our five-star hotel, can we?'

He gently swabbed the blood and matter from Anna's cheek and tried not to stare into her green eyes as he tipped more water onto his t-shirt and swept it over her collarbone and shoulder.

'There you go. Much better.' He smiled.

'Any excuse to get your shirt off, isn't it?' said Mitch.

Dan threw the empty water bottle at the back of Mitch's head and heard a satisfying smack as it bounced off.

'No respect,' muttered Mitch, as Dan and Anna laughed.

FORTY-FIVE

Thirteen hours later, Dan swung the vehicle to a standstill on a roadside promontory, braking to a stop at the steel barrier that gave way to a steep ridge at the edge of the small Spanish-held coastal enclave of Ceuta.

He'd swapped over with Mitch two hours ago, letting his colleague stretch his legs in the passenger seat and make a call to David and Mel as soon as they were within easy reach of their final destination. Dan thought it wise to keep their plans to themselves until the last minute, worried their position would be intercepted before he'd had a chance to get Anna to safety once and for all.

Despite his concerns, their journey out of the dunes had been uneventful, and both Mitch and

Anna had fallen asleep to the drone of the pock-marked asphalt of the northern route passing under the wheels of the four-wheel drive. Anna had remained in slumber as he'd stopped the vehicle on the side of the road an hour ago to refuel the tank from two of the fuel canisters he and Mitch had liberated from the Russians' vehicles earlier that day.

'Do you think she'll be okay once she gets away from here?' Mitch had asked.

Dan had looked up from his position at the rear of the vehicle as he lowered the now-empty jerry can and peered through the back window at Anna's slumbering form.

She'd curled up across the back seat, her features peaceful.

'I think so,' he'd said. 'Her father will make sure of it – and her mother is amazing.' His mouth quirked. 'Actually, I'm pretty sure she's going to be okay.'

Now, he leaned on the steering wheel, his eyes roaming the layout of the town sprawled out beneath their position, the late afternoon sun casting a dappled pink light across the roofs and terraces of the small Spanish enclave.

Anna yawned as she pulled herself upright and leaned between the front seats. 'Are we there?'

'Yes. It's only a ten-minute drive from here to the hotel where we're meeting David and Mel,' said Mitch.

They sat in silence for a moment, savouring the view.

Dan chuckled. 'I don't know about you two, but I could murder a cold beer.'

Anna groaned. 'I've been dreaming about a hot bath,' she murmured. 'What are we waiting for?'

Dan grinned and released the handbrake, steering the vehicle back to the road. 'Come on then.'

The road dropped through a short series of narrow switchbacks until levelling out at the bottom of the hill, where the urban sprawl of the port town encroached.

Mitch navigated using his smartphone, and they found the hotel with ease.

Dan slowed, applied the handbrake, and got out, tossing the keys to the bewildered parking valet who was staring at Dan's state of undress, his eyes wide.

'Y-you can't park there,' he stammered. 'It's for paying guests only, not backpackers!'

Mitch roared with laughter as he helped Anna from the four-wheel drive. 'Bad luck, pal – we *are* paying guests.'

Dan grinned at the valet, then joined Mitch and Anna at the wide double doors to the hotel. He glanced down at the assortment of paperwork Anna clutched to her chest that she'd liberated from the Russians' vehicles. 'Got everything?'

'Yes. Thank you,' she said. She placed a hand on his arm. 'Thank you for everything, Dan. And you, Mitch.'

Dan nodded.

'Taylor? Are you actually lost for words?' said Mitch.

'I think he is,' said Anna, smiling.

'Right,' said Mitch, and held the door open for them to pass through. 'In that case, last one to the bar buys the drinks.'

FORTY-SIX

Dan climbed out of the chauffeured car David had procured from the hotel concierge and slowly pivoted on his toes, his eyes searching for any potential danger amongst the silhouetted cars parked beside the entrance to the arrivals lounge of the international airport.

Once satisfied there were no imminent threats, he bent down, pulled a backpack from the passenger seat, and beckoned to Anna. 'Okay, come on. We're good to go.'

Upon arriving at the hotel, Anna had joined Dan and Mitch at the bar for a drink before she started leafing through the papers she'd retrieved from the military enterpriser's vehicle.

Dan had grinned at her persistence. 'You've got your investigator look going on,' he'd said.

She'd smiled back before excusing herself and then spending half an hour in the hotel's business centre studiously writing out all her notes and compiling a substantial record of the past few days' events for David before allowing herself the luxury of the hot bath she'd craved.

When David and Mel had arrived, they'd been delighted with Anna's progress. Accompanied by the photographs Mitch had taken of the dead Russian mercenaries, it gave them a head start on working with her employer in Rotterdam and other security agencies to hunt down the architects behind the attempted coup.

Mel had arranged flights for Anna back to the United States that same evening, correctly guessing that General Collins would be desperate to see his daughter after finding out Dan had brought her safely to the Spanish territory.

Now, Dan placed his hand gently at Anna's elbow and steered her towards the automatic glass doors and into the air-conditioned building.

With no luggage to check-in, Anna's seat was confirmed without delay, and Dan led her through the concourse to a café near the departure gates.

As they sat, he slipped the brand new backpack off his shoulder and handed it to her.

'Mel put some things together for you,' he said, 'to make the trip home a bit more comfortable.'

Anna nodded and peered inside, her lip quivering. 'Tell her I said, "thank you"?'

'Of course.'

Sitting so close to her, his senses flared at the scent of the hotel's complimentary soap and shampoo she'd used. He'd used the same, but on Anna, it seemed to blossom, filling the air between them.

He cleared his throat. 'So, what's the first thing you're going to do when you get home?'

Anna laughed, and Dan's heart lurched as he realised it was the first time he'd heard her let her guard down so completely over the past five days.

'I think I'm going to have another bath,' she said. She slapped his arm playfully. 'Don't laugh – I swear I can still feel sand everywhere.'

Dan chuckled. 'Yeah, I know what you mean.'

'What about you?' Anna pointed at the list of flights displayed on the departure boards. 'Where are you going next?'

'I don't know,' he said truthfully, then shrugged. 'I'm sure I'll think of something.'

Dan stayed with her until the moment the flight

was called and walked with her to the departure gate.

Movement to his left caught his eye, and he reached out for Anna's arm, pulling her to a stop.

She turned to him, her eyes wide. 'What is it?'

Dan smiled. 'There's someone here to see you,' he said, and pointed.

The tall form of General Bartholomew 'Bart' Collins stood in the doorway to a private room off the concourse, his imposing form dwarfing the airline representative that appeared at his side.

Although his silver hair still resembled a military crop, his face was etched with the stress of the past week waiting for news of his daughter, and his eyes were bloodshot.

'Dad?'

Anna let out a whimper and crossed the corridor, her father's arms wrapping around her as she burst into tears.

Dan lowered his gaze. He could tell the general was struggling to keep his emotions in check in front of him, and knew he'd be an emotional wreck if it had been a kid of his in the same situation.

'Dan,' the general managed to choke. 'I don't know how I'll ever repay you.'

Dan glanced up and met the man's eye. 'You don't have to,' he said.

'Any time you need me, you ask, understand?'

The man's stare bore into him as he held out his hand, and Dan nodded, shaking it.

'I will, thanks.'

'What are you doing here?' Anna said, taking a paper tissue from the airline representative and wiping her eyes.

'I couldn't wait until you got back home,' said Collins. 'I had to come.'

The airline representative cleared his throat. 'I'm sorry, sir, but you need to board the plane.'

'Of course.'

The general took his daughter's hand and smiled. 'Let's get you home.'

Anna turned to Dan and seemed to be lost for words.

He closed the distance between them and pulled her into his arms. 'It's over,' he said.

'Thank you,' she whispered.

They turned at the voice of the airline representative, who frowned and pointed at his watch.

'Go,' said Dan. 'Say "hi" to your mom for me.'

Anna pulled away and squeezed his hand, tears welling up in her eyes.

'Miss? You need to board,' called the airline staff member. 'We're going to close the gate now.'

Dan gave Anna a small push. 'Go on. I'll talk to you on the phone in a few days, let you know what we're up to, if I can.'

'Okay.'

Dan stood with his arms crossed, watching until Anna had followed her father through the departure gate, until she'd disappeared from sight.

He wandered over to the floor-to-ceiling window and waited as the aircraft pulled away from the gate, taxied across to its allocated position, and lined up for take-off.

He didn't move until the plane was safely in the air, its navigation lights a mere speck in the night sky.

FORTY-SEVEN

Dan excused himself from the small group at the table, pushed open the door to the sweeping balcony of the hotel's restaurant, and rested his bottle of beer on a table overlooking the town.

Salty sea air filled his senses, and he took a deep breath, filling his lungs.

He wandered over to the edge of the hotel restaurant's balcony and rested his forearms on the rail while he collected his thoughts.

David had already made it clear that he wouldn't be participating in the hunt for the people who tried to organise the coup; it would be handed over to another agency that had a long reach into Eastern Europe and beyond.

Dan pulled out the photograph the Russian had

handed to him and gritted his teeth. Somehow, he had to convince David to include him. He had a message to deliver.

He glanced over his shoulder at the sound of the balcony door opening to see Mel walking towards him, a glass of wine in her hand, and tucked the photograph away.

She placed her wine on the table next to his beer bottle and then joined him at the rail.

'Penny for your thoughts?'

Dan's mouth quirked. 'You don't think they're worth more than that?'

Mel smiled. 'Not in today's economy. The department's watching its finances too closely.'

'I'll bet.'

Mel sighed. 'Thinking about your boat?'

'Yeah. And where I'm going to live now.'

'You've still got the house outside Oxford?'

Dan nodded. 'I just don't know if I'm ready to go back yet, Mel. I kind of liked being on the water.' He straightened, turned his back to the view, and crossed his arms over his chest. 'What have you found out about the explosion? Do you know who's responsible?'

Mel's gaze dropped to the floor. 'Yes,' she said. 'But David wants to talk to you about that himself.'

She raised her eyes to meet his. 'So, please, wait to speak to him, okay?'

Dan frowned and then shrugged. 'Okay. When?'

Mel peered over her shoulder. David and Mitch were still deep in conversation at the table, seemingly oblivious to their missing colleagues. 'Soon.'

'Why can't you tell me?'

Mel smiled. 'Because I don't have all the facts yet – David was still checking some things out and waiting on some phone calls. I also know what your temper can be like.'

Dan conceded the point and gestured towards the table. 'Might as well finish these while we wait.'

He pulled out a chair for Mel, waited until she was seated, then sat next to her, both of them drifting into a companionable silence as the warm night air carried the sound of cicadas from the trees below.

Dan took a swig from his beer bottle and ran his hand over the condensation-soaked label. 'Have you spoken to Sarah?'

'She knows you're safe.'

'Thank you.'

His on-again, off-again lover would probably kill him when she saw him, especially after he'd had to leave England in such a hurry and had avoided all contact with her in case he endangered her.

'She also asked me when you might return. I told her that was up to you.'

Dan grunted, his eyes flickering to the older of the two men who sat inside. 'I don't want to come back, just to get arrested or face another inquiry.' He sighed. 'Life was so much simpler before all this.'

Mel leaned forward and rested her hand on the back of his. 'From what I heard, you were drinking yourself into a hole.' She squeezed his hand. 'I think you like complicated.'

Dan raised an eyebrow and took another sip from his beer. 'Maybe.'

She chuckled, removed her hand, and picked up her wine glass, her eyes seeking out the yacht masts that rose above the marina beyond the north of the town. 'Whatever you say, boss.'

Dan had to smile. He'd only been working with Mel a short while before he'd left England in a hurry, but he was impressed by her intuition.

'So, what have you been up to while I've been sailing around the Med?' he asked. 'Apart from spying on me?'

She had the decency to choke on her wine. 'I

wasn't *spying*,' she insisted. 'I was just, you know, keeping an eye on you.'

'Of course.' Dan grinned. 'So, spill it. What's been going on?'

'Well, we're obviously keeping an eye on developments in Russia,' said Mel. 'Although this attempted coup caught us off guard.' She shook her head. 'We were lucky Anna and her colleague worked out what was happening so quickly.' She put down her glass. 'There are some who think Russia will implode over the coming years – splinter into smaller states, all of whom will probably pick a fight with each other.'

Dan grimaced. 'That's not good. The current leadership is difficult to deal with at the best of times, without separate factions all chasing their own agendas.'

'Quite. And then there's the Middle East, of course,' said Mel. 'And goodness knows where that's going to lead. What with that and Asia, I think we're going to be kept busy for a while yet.'

She broke off as the door to the balcony opened.

David appeared, closely followed by Mitch, who balanced a collection of freshly poured drinks in his hands. David waited until he'd joined Mel and Dan at the table and then locked the door, preventing anyone else from exiting the restaurant in their wake.

Dan waited until everyone had settled, then took the fresh cold bottle of beer Mitch handed to him, and eyed David.

'So, who blew up my boat?'

FORTY-EIGHT

David shot a warning glance at Mel, who ignored him and sipped her wine, her legs crossed, one foot bouncing in the air.

Dan frowned as Mitch edged a little further away from his right, and recalled Mel's comment about his temper. He turned his attention back to David.

'Well?'

'It took a while to get the forensics from what was left of the boat,' began David. 'But we've managed to retrieve some of the components that *might* have been used to fix the bomb to the bottom of your boat. You can imagine the state they're in. We also found CCTV footage from the bank you'd used to get the money out to pay for the replacement fuel pump,' he added. 'And it looks like you were being followed.'

Dan frowned. 'But I've been checking for tails,' he argued. 'I've seen no-one.'

'This guy got lucky,' said Mitch. 'Trust me, he wasn't a professional – he wouldn't have been caught on camera otherwise.'

'Do you know who he is?'

'Nasir Abbas,' said David. 'Basically, he's a gun for hire. Algerian by birth, but he's cropped up all over the Mediterranean – he tends to work for whoever happens to be paying him that day. No allegiances.'

'Do you know who hired him?'

David sighed. 'Yes. Harith Gulzar.'

Dan's mind worked as he tried to recall where he'd heard the name before. It sounded familiar, yet...

He shook his head. 'I don't understand.'

'Harith Gulzar is Yasmin Gulzar's older brother,' said David softly. 'You knew her as Antonia Almasi.'

Dan pushed his chair back from the table and stalked across the balcony to the railing.

He wrapped his fingers around the cool steel

and closed his eyes, blood rushing to his head as the shock of David's revelation began to sink in.

Antonia's brother?

He groaned, the memories painful. The betrayal by a beautiful Iranian agent had cost the life of one of the team, and he'd never forgiven himself.

Was this to be his future? Dealing with a man who sought revenge for his sister's death?

He turned to find three worried faces staring back at him and exhaled, trying to lose some of the tension that cramped his shoulders.

'Come and sit down,' said David. 'I'll bring you up to speed.'

He pulled a folded sheaf of papers from the inside pocket of his linen jacket and lay them out on the table so the whole team could see.

'Gulzar is a computer prodigy,' he began. 'More so than his sister.' He pointed to the first page. 'This is a copy of a communiqué from the Saudi embassy in Washington.' He looked up to the three pairs of eyes watching him intently. 'The Saudis believe Gulzar is going to mount an imminent attack on American soil and sent a copy of their warning to London as well. Their belief is that if Gulzar is successful in the United States, then England will be next.'

'What is it with that family?' said Mitch, rubbing his chin.

'I said he was a computer prodigy,' said David. 'I didn't say he was sane.'

'The Americans have stepped up checks on their infrastructure?'

David nodded at Dan. 'Yes, but Gulzar is clever,' he said. 'And we don't want to take any chances. The British government want to get their hands on Gulzar before the Americans do. And, given we have a lot more information about that family on our files than they do, we stand a very good chance of stopping whatever it is he's got planned.'

Dan tapped his fingers on the table, an uneven rhythm. His mind raced. Was he ready to work with David again?

He glared at Mitch, who for once remained silent.

'No wise cracks?'

Mitch shook his head and folded his arms across his chest.

'Mel?'

The analyst shrugged. 'Your call, boss.'

'All right,' said Dan. He turned to David. 'I'm in,' he said. 'But on one condition.'

'What?'

'I want to finish what we started here. I want to go to Russia.'

'You've already been cleared for action,' said David. He leaned across the table and held out his hand.

'Welcome back, Dan.'

FORTY-NINE

Two weeks later

North Moscow

Dan checked over his shoulder as the front door to the apartment opened, then returned his attention to the building opposite his position, the wheels from a packed commuter tram squealing against its rails as it turned the corner and disappeared from sight.

He rubbed his hands together, the apartment heating having been turned off by the utility company when the last owner had left some six months previously. A heavy downpour lashed the window while a northerly wind shook the pane in its frame.

A brown paper bag appeared next to his elbow, and his stomach rumbled, despite the monotony of the diet he and Mitch had adopted the past few days.

'Great. More Pirozhki,' he muttered, and then sighed. 'Thanks, Tim.'

'No problem.'

Dan turned to face the British-born agent. 'Anything to report?'

The man pulled a hat from his head, sending a spray of water across the linoleum floor, tossed it onto the table, then shrugged his jacket off his shoulders and hung it over the back of a chair. 'All quiet out there,' he said. 'What about here?'

'She turned up an hour ago as usual,' said Mitch, helping himself to the second of the bags Tim had placed on the table. 'Regular as clockwork.'

Dan checked his watch, a new model he'd purchased on his way through Heathrow before he and Mitch had caught separate flights into the former Soviet Union. 'You're sure he's here on Thursdays?'

Tim nodded and took a large bite of Pirozhki

before responding. 'We've had an eye on him for a while,' he said, and then grinned. 'Just been waiting for an opportunity to do something about him.'

Dan exhaled, unwrapped the top of the paper bag, and fished out another one of the meat-filled pastries, then returned his attention to the street below while he chewed.

He pushed back his chair, leaned forward, and peered through the rifle scope that was trained on an apartment on the sixth floor of the concrete structure.

A gap in the net curtains allowed a view of sumptuous furnishings; décor splashed across the walls in hues of red and pink, and mirrors added light to an otherwise dull space. A fake chandelier hung from the ceiling, the light bulbs casting shadows into the corners of the room.

A woman pranced into view, naked except for a pair of black lace knickers, her head thrown back as she laughed. She moved across the room, then pulled a man into view, his gut hanging over his boxer shorts doing little to hide the erection that pushed at the fabric.

'Busy girl,' Mitch commented through a mouthful of food.

Dan moved away from the scope and checked

his watch. 'She is.' He took a bite of Pirozhki. 'Guess it pays well.'

'She's a favourite with a lot of the government ministers,' said Miles. 'Not to mention some of the foreign diplomats.'

Mitch shook his head. 'Shame we can't get a listening device in the room.'

'What's to say we haven't?' said Tim.

Dan choked on his food. 'Really?'

Tim inclined his head.

'Bloody hell.'

Upon their arrival in the country, Dan and Mitch had kept a low profile while David and Mel worked with the other British security agencies, gathering intelligence about the man who had employed the military enterpriser and devising a plan to deal with him, once and for all.

They had taken the name Abramov had given to Dan in his last dying moments and had traced Kozlov's current whereabouts with vigour.

Luckily, Sergei Kozlov was already known to the British establishment.

He had visited arms fairs in London on several occasions, legitimately purchasing weapons on behalf of the Russian government. He had wined and dined with minor royalty and charmed his way into the upper echelons of British society.

And, on the side, he had quietly siphoned off weapons from each shipment of arms sent to the mother country, stockpiling a cache for a small private army of mercenaries that only served to do his bidding, and that of the state's puppet-masters.

Both Dan and Mitch had fought down the impatience that came with an impending operation; they knew when the time was right, they'd be put into action.

After his involvement in the attempted coup in Western Sahara had become apparent, together with the weapons thefts, it hadn't taken much persuasion to convince the Prime Minister that Kozlov was about to become a major embarrassment for him.

The orders were released without delay.

That call had come from David four days earlier, and within two hours they'd met up with Tim Fallon, a young British agent who ran several safe houses around the Russian capital.

At once, the team of three had moved into position, taking up residence in an abandoned apartment the secret service had kept under wraps for over a year.

Tim's admission that the apartment in the building opposite had been fitted with listening devices confirmed Dan's original suspicions – all the time the woman entertained the higher echelons of the Russian government, her presence in the building was assured, and her life along with it. He wondered if she was aware that she was currently the centre of the British intelligence agencies' attention.

Mitch joined Dan at the window and folded his arms across his chest as the previous customer stepped from the apartment block and raised a black umbrella to ward off the rain.

He hurried across the road to a waiting car, whereupon the driver emerged and opened the back door, taking the umbrella from the man as he squeezed his large bulk into the back seat.

Once his passenger was settled, the driver closed the door, retracted the umbrella, and gave the street a cursory glance before taking his seat behind the wheel and pulling the car into the flow of traffic.

Dan checked his watch again, fighting the adrenalin rush that threatened to shred his nerves.

Five minutes later, Mitch rocked forward on his toes. 'Next,' he said, and jerked his head towards a figure walking towards the apartment from the opposite direction.

Tim joined them. 'This is our man.'

'Where's his car?' said Dan.

'He has his driver drop him off two streets away,' said Tim. 'Prefers to walk, and then the car picks him up outside the building afterwards.'

'Risky,' said Mitch.

Tim shrugged. 'As a politician in Moscow, everything is risky.'

Dan ignored them both and instead narrowed his eyes as he observed the man approaching the building.

As Kozlov strode up the steps and entered the apartment building, Dan exhaled and moved back to his position at the rifle.

He settled his eye socket against the scope and concentrated on his breathing, his finger on the trigger guard.

'Our man has entered the building,' said Mitch. 'You should see her open the door to him in about forty seconds if the elevator's clear.'

'Count it down,' said Dan.

Silence enveloped the room as the three men waited expectantly, before Mitch's voice cut the air.

'Three. Two. One.'

A heartbeat later, Dan watched through the scope as the woman in the apartment walked past the window, a satin robe draped around her body, and moved to the front door. A moment later, she returned, leading the man towards the bedroom at the right of the apartment and out of sight of Dan's position.

'Based on intel, they'll be in the bedroom for about fifteen minutes, and then she'll serve him brandy in the living room,' said Tim, a pair of binoculars to his eyes. 'That's when you'll get your clear shot.'

A moment later, Mitch swore. 'What the hell is she doing?'

The prostitute had reappeared, peered through the window to the street below, and then pulled the curtains closed.

'What the fuck?'

Tim's words echoed what was going through Dan's mind at the exact same time.

'She's never done that before,' the British agent said. 'Christ, what a fuck up.'

Dan swore and pushed himself away from the rifle.

'Pack this up. Get ready to roll,' he said, and grabbed his jacket, pushing his pistol into his belt loop and tucking his shirt down.

Tim cornered him at the door. 'Wait – what are you doing?'

'I came here to do a job,' said Dan. He pointed towards the building opposite. 'I reckon I've got about twenty minutes before Kozlov's official car picks him up, right?'

The agent nodded.

'Right,' said Dan. He reached into his belt loop for the pistol tucked under his shirt, checked the magazine, and slammed it back into place before glaring at Tim. 'This is the only chance we've got,' he said. 'If we don't stop him, we're always going to have the risk of a coup hanging over our heads.'

'There has to be another way,' insisted the agent. 'You'll never get away with this.'

Dan pointed at the agent. 'I will, because you're going to turn off the microphones in that apartment, do you understand me?' His mouth quirked. 'After that, it's probably time you went back to the office,' he said. He checked over his shoulder.

Mitch had dismantled the rifle, put the components into a duffel bag, and now stood in the middle of the room, his eyes darting between Dan and Tim.

'Are we going, or what?' he demanded.

Dan faced Tim. 'Clear out,' he said, and punched the man's shoulder. 'We'll take it from here. You never saw us.'

Tim sighed and stepped to one side. 'For Christ's sake, be careful.'

Dan winked and led Mitch into the hallway, breaking into a run.

He pushed open the emergency exit door and ran down the stairs, Mitch's footsteps in his wake.

At the bottom, he slowed, opened the fire door a crack, and checked the way was clear.

'Give me two minutes,' he said. 'If we both run, people will notice. I'll meet you outside the front door.'

'Copy that.'

Despite being early summer in the city, a chill clung to the air, and for a moment Dan couldn't fathom whether it was real or imagined. The enormity of their task hadn't left him since his arrival four days ago.

He tugged his collar up and launched himself across the street, dodged between a car and a cyclist, and hurried up the stone steps to the apartment block he'd been staring at for the past four days.

He knew the layout intimately. Tim had provided copies of construction drawings, and in between stints watching the building and monitoring its occupants, he'd studied every line of the architect's handiwork.

He had hoped they wouldn't need to step inside the building itself; Tim was right – it was risky.

If one of the other residents spotted him before he'd had a chance to complete his mission, he and Mitch would be compromised.

They'd planned for contingencies as much as possible; Mitch had parked around the corner from the building they'd been hiding in for the past four days, and Tim had made a point to check their escape route hadn't been tampered with each time he'd left the apartment to fetch food.

Tim had ensured he'd built up a presence at the apartment in the two days leading up to Dan and Mitch's arrival, his fluent Russian tinged with the right amount of local dialect so as not to raise suspicions amongst his new neighbours, and his cover story was water-tight.

Dan and Mitch had arrived under cover of darkness, easily avoiding detection on the security cameras after Tim had disconnected them remotely; the circuit would be returned to normal on their departure.

Now, he pushed through the entrance door and stepped into a long narrow foyer. Ignoring the two elevators to his left, he took the stairs, keeping his step light.

As he reached the landing for the sixth floor, he took a few seconds to get his breathing under control before striding towards the door to the prostitute's apartment.

His Russian was atrocious, but he hoped to instil a sense of panic in the woman and indignation in the politician.

'Here goes,' he muttered, drew his weapon, and hammered on the door.

Nothing happened.

He waited a few seconds and then repeated the action, shouting at the top of his voice to open the door.

The woman's voice sounded through the wooden surface, her tone both angry and confused.

Dan stilled his breathing as he heard her approach the door, his fingers tightening the suppressor to the barrel of his weapon, and then her voice became pacifying as she told her client to wait in the bedroom, and the sound of the chain being removed reached his ears.

The door opened a crack, and Dan used all his weight to drive it open, sending the woman stumbling backwards across the carpeted living area.

'Don't scream,' he said, aiming the gun at her.

Her eyes wide, she shook her head.

'Where is he?'

She raised a trembling hand and pointed to the bedroom.

'Okay, go.' Dan pointed at the door. 'Go. Don't come back.'

He kept his gun pointed at the bedroom door while she scurried across the floor, gathering her clothes, pulling her jeans on, and wrapping a coat around her shoulders.

She whimpered as she brushed past him on the way to the door, then snatched her handbag from a small table next to him, and fled.

Dan kicked the door shut in her wake and crossed the room.

The aroma of cheap perfume and incense sticks clung to the air, while candles burned on a coffee table under the window.

He reminded himself he was trying to kill the very successful leader of a group of mercenaries – someone who was, in all likelihood, armed.

That man was also, in all likelihood, placing a call on a mobile phone, seeking help from his men.

Dan swung round the door frame to the bedroom, gun raised.

Sergei Kozlov sat on the bed, the phone to his ear, his mouth gaping as his soft white gut escaped from his open cotton shirt and pooled over his boxer shorts.

Dan didn't hesitate.

The shot caught Kozlov in the chest, sending him tumbling over the double bed, blood splatter covering the satin sheets.

Dan reached over, picked up the mobile from where it had fallen, and ended the call, ignoring the Russian's fingers as they clawed the air, trying to reach the phone.

Kozlov's mouth moved, his eyes wide as his dying breath cursed the man who had shot him.

Dan waited a second, then raised the gun once more and shot the Russian between the eyes.

His head jerked up at the sound of a motorcycle revving outside the building.

He'd agreed with Mitch that he was to wait only one minute, and if Dan didn't show up, then he was to leave – immediately.

Time to go.

He hurried towards the bedroom door before pausing and reaching under his jacket.

He turned back, bent over the dead Russian, and then placed the photograph of Abramov's daughter into the man's shirt pocket.

'Job done,' he murmured.

THE END

FROM THE AUTHOR

Dear Reader,

First of all, I wanted to say a huge thank you for choosing to read *Behind the Wire*, the fourth book in the *Dan Taylor* series. I hope you enjoyed the story.

If you did enjoy it, I'd be grateful if you could write a review. It doesn't have to be long, just a few words, but it is the best way for me to help new readers discover one of my books for the first time.

If you'd like to stay up to date with my new releases, as well as exclusive competitions and giveaways, you're welcome to join my Reader Group at my website, www.rachelamphlett.com. I will never share your email address, and you can unsubscribe at any time. You can also contact me via Facebook, Twitter, or by email. I love hearing from readers – I read every message and will always reply.

Thanks again for your support.

Best wishes,

Rachel Amphlett

Printed in Great Britain
by Amazon

26419918R00209